The
Architect

Jack Carnegie

Copyright © 2021 by Jack Carnegie

The right of Jack Carnegie to be identified as the author of this work has been asserted in accordance with the Copyright, Designs and Patents Act 1988.

All rights reserved.

This book or any portion thereof may not be reproduced or used in any manner whatsoever without the express written permission of the author.

This is a work of fiction. Names, characters, places, organisations, events and incidents are either the products of the author's imagination or are used fictitiously. Any resemblance to actual persons, living or dead, businesses, companies, events, or locales is entirely coincidental.

ISBN: 9798487896773

Acknowledgements

Paul Addy

Dedication

To my partner, Carol, and to our dog, Max, both of whom are the best inspirations a man could ever have.

Cover by Jack Carnegie

Chapter 1

The Continuous Solution

I was looking for a new job, I wasn't enjoying the NYPD anymore, the work I was doing had little to no interest to me; I'd seen it all and wanted a fresh start. The advert in the New York Times had been headed, *Detective wanted to work on historical files.*

I phoned and spoke to a Mr Janowitz who asked me a few questions about my employment. I told him I was a badged Detective currently going nowhere and needed a new direction. He asked about my pay grade then said he could better it if I passed the interview and background checks. He told me he'd been a cop himself in Greenwich and made Detective. From there on in, we spoke about the job in general and he invited me to his home for an interview. He told me he had another employee, an Irishman named Findlay Quinn who'd served as a cop in the Bronx; I'd work alongside him if I got the job. "Let's see if we get on together first though," he said.

He seemed like a nice guy on the phone, someone I could talk honestly to, which was important to me. I'd worked with some unscrupulous characters over the years and hitting a benchmark at fifty had made me reconsider my life, I wanted more than a job that made me feel I was working in a factory. I'd said the wrong things to the wrong people at the wrong time and now all I investigated was the mounting pile of dead-end 'write offs' that filled my desk. That was the reason I'd first looked into the situations vacant column, I guess I needed a challenge, something I could get my teeth into and thought maybe historical crimes would interest me, it would be different at the very least. I wasn't married so had no real family commitments, although my girlfriend Jody would say differently.

We lived together in an apartment in The Flat Iron Building off 5th and East 22nd. I'd been lucky; I'd bought it before the roof blew off the housing market. I'd taken the leap when everyone else was renting and had it paid off within ten years when the overtime had been endless. It'd been a good investment, practically 'free' accommodation for the last fifteen years, although the service charges had rocketed in the years since I first bought it. It staggered me how much folk were paying for their rent these days, an outrageous sum of money I thought, I'd often considered retiring, renting it out and using my pension to buy a place in the country. Ideas for my old age, but I still had something inside me I needed to do, work that actually meant something. I was done with just being a New York cop, I wanted to prove myself and I had the financial stability to do that. It hadn't always been that way though, as a young cop I'd struggled trying to keep those mortgage payments up, but then I'd earned my detective's badge, had a couple of 'lucky break' cases and made the homicide squad. Fortunately, people never got tired of killing each other.

A deposit gifted to me by my folks came in handy also. Originally, the apartment was just somewhere I could unwind and lay my head, but then Jody came along and really made it a home, doing the things only a woman could.

On the Monday of the interview, I took the Metro north to Greenwich, travelling from the 23rd Street subway towards Stamford, coming out over the Third Avenue Bridge and crossing the Harlem River, arriving in Greenwich at nineteen minutes past the hour. Schedules interested me, the Metro ran like clockwork, Mussolini himself would have been proud of the precision. The interview was at midday, giving me ample time to find Janowitz's address in Idar Court.

I'd been to Greenwich before, a nice town I thought, one I could settle into myself because it just felt like time slowed down there; everything seemed to travel at light speed in the 'Big Apple'.

It would be an eight-minute walk to the house, so I killed the time buying a newspaper from the stand and a coffee in the station café.

I found his place off Sound View Drive, a dog leg to the left and there you were. A few houses up, I entered a driveway which took me across sandstone pavers to the front door. Knocking, I found myself unnaturally tense and nervous; suddenly realising it'd been over twenty years since I'd sat an interview for a job. A woman answered the door; I assumed it was Janowitz's wife.

"Hello, can I help you?" she asked, flashing me a lovely smile. I told her why I was there, and she asked me to step on in.

"I'm Luiza, I'll just get him for you, he's in the tunnel," she said, which confused me somewhat, it was only later I found out he called his study 'Harry' after the tunnel in the film, *The Great Escape*. I guessed it was a family thing.

"Hello, I'm Emil, you must be Eugene Kennedy, come on through to the study," he said in a welcoming manner. Luiza asked if I'd like a tea or coffee. "Tea, one sugar, no milk, thanks," I confirmed.

We sat in the study and he tried to make me feel relaxed, telling me what the job entailed and what I could expect regarding the workload. He asked me about family, I told him I had a girlfriend named Jody, no children and an apartment on Fifth Avenue. He asked me to call him Emil.

"Let's cut to the chase, Eugene," he said. "Take a look at this file, Quinn's working on this as we speak. I really need him to concentrate his efforts, see what you make of it, he could do with a little help," he said, enthusiastically waving a file in the air before handing it to me.

I opened it. Inside the first page was a photograph of a dreary looking woman, the owner of a chin that reminded me of Jay Leno. She had deep-set eyes and a mean mouth. Her name was Ilse Gerver. She'd been a guard in the Nazi camps who'd escaped the noose by chance. The prosecution hadn't submitted sufficient evidence against her at the time, so she was given just ten years imprisonment and an early release whilst her colleagues were hung by the neck by a British executioner, a guy named Pierrepoint. I thought his name sounded French. When I'd finished, I looked up and simply said, "You've got my interest."

Emil let me know that Luiza had buried herself in a project they'd set up together, a foundation for the victims of the Holocaust they called 'The Sikora Foundation' named after a little bird he'd seen at Auschwitz when he was an inmate. He explained, "He always seemed to arrive when death came calling, a sort of guardian into the next life. We thought 'The Aleksy Markowski Foundation' was a bit of a mouthful." I didn't understand but allowed him to continue.

He told me they'd set it up to help any surviving victims that might need support or assistance in their old age. "It was something Aleksy would have wanted and been proud of," he added.

Luiza was passionate about the project, reiterating Emil's points, sometimes ending his sentences for him.

Meanwhile, Emil had collated all the information he could about Ilse Gerver and told me, "Justice has to knock on her door at some stage. She should have been shown the noose by Pierrepoint but instead, she got off lightly. What this possibly means is we can go for her on the evidence that wasn't presented at the time of the earlier trial. I've received the original court notes and there was, I think, sufficient case to argue for retrial," he said.

He'd given Quinn a list naming several female guards to acquaint himself with some weeks earlier, at first the Irishman focussed on Hertha Bothe, one of several female SS Guards in the files, but he found her situation too problematic and eventually it was Gerver's history that drew his interest most of all.

"He told me, there was just something pure evil about her, it needed his sole attention, so I gave him permission to concentrate his efforts on Gerver alone, effectively he took over the court proceedings against her. When he read the crimes she'd committed, he couldn't believe she hadn't been hung."

Emil had told Quinn that at the original trial a survivor had come forward from Bergen-Belsen, saying he'd witnessed Gerver beat a Hungarian Jew to death with a wooden block and another had witnessed her shoot two prisoners. "These are people we can use," he said. I nodded, replying, "If they're still alive that is."

A wan smile of agreement wandered across his mouth. "It's not much to go on, Eugene, but you'll find Quinn is relentless with his investigations. He more than proved himself in the Ernst Schaefer case, taking control of the situation when all looked lost. He made himself a valuable asset to my work on the files and you won't go far wrong learning a few tricks from him," he said with obvious pride.

He went on to explain to me that before he'd died Markowski had entrusted him with a considerable library of files and asked that he bring to justice as many war criminals as he possibly could.

"I work most days on the files, taking weekends off with Luiza, I thought that only fair to her," he informed me. "In effect I want you to take on my role, to allow me more time with my wife. I'll still be involved, just not as much as before, time's catching up with me and I want to live out the remaining years of my life in peace, but I can't abandon this quest, I owe it to Aleksy," he said and I understood, he deserved that from what he'd told me so far about his life.

I was interested; it looked like work that would test me, something that might relight a passion I'd once had.

He told me of the Ernst Schaefer case, giving me details about the German rat runs and the alleged 73 tons of gold stolen from the victims of the Holocaust. "It was enough to keep a Venezuelan dictator in power for decades." He spoke with disgust on his face. I recalled the name and realised I'd seen in the news that Schaefer had been shot. It was in the New York Times a few months earlier, a small column with a headline 'Former Nazi Shot Dead.' It was an article that didn't adequately reflect what Emil was now telling me.

"Schaefer and his Nazi pals gifted gold plundered from the dead to the Venezuelan dictator and in return, he provided them with a haven and the lifestyle of the rich and powerful." He looked me squarely in the eyes. "The Nazis extracted gold from the mouths of the people they murdered then used their bodies in commercial processes, Eugene. Justice has to be served for each and every one of them."

In his words and eyes, I saw his sadness and passion. I was to find out why. He'd been a prisoner in Auschwitz between 1943 and 1945 and his whole family had been murdered by the regime. I could see the pain etched on his face as he told me about the individual circumstances in which his family had met their deaths, it was humbling to listen to the man. I sat quietly, his history opening up to me, a total stranger. When he'd finished, there was an awkward silence. I didn't know what to say. To be honest, I felt more emotional than I wanted to.

Emil broke the moment. "Quinn has been researching the first report into the Ilse Gerver case. He's found a man called 'Wilhelm Becker' who'd testified against Gerver but there are others, not known at the time of the original trial. Interestingly and importantly, all of them identify Rudi Baumann as the SS guard in overall charge of her at Belsen." He spoke as if he had some sort of prior knowledge of Baumann and saw the hint of query in my face. "Whenever an SS guard comes to my attention, I make notes, I save them all in a file for future use, you just never know. Anyway, Wilhelm Becker had testified he'd seen Gerver shoot at female prisoners who were carrying food containers from the kitchen to the block. Also, the court transcripts revealed Gerver was accused of beating and kicking prisoners so badly it resulted, ultimately, in their deaths."

He'd sold it to me; it didn't seem like a job he was offering me, more of a mission. I *wanted* to bring Ilse Gerver to justice, she'd be totally unaware of the work being collated against her all these years later, so she was living on borrowed time.

Emil smiled. "These were the sort of cases Aleksy would have wanted me to investigate, ones that had slipped through the system. Surprisingly, it was quite often the case."

He placed photographs on the table, carefully positioning links between names, compiling the evidence in a sequence he knew I would understand. "It's how I always worked when I was in the job," he said. I used the same techniques in homicide; it seemed we were cut from the same cloth.

"Slowly the case against Gerver is coming together, Quinn has it all in hand, she'll be sat at home none the wiser to the years of evidence compiled against her, going about her daily business as if none of her crimes had ever taken place. It's how the Nazis work, they wipe their memories clean of all the atrocities and crimes they committed," he said. I nodded in agreement.

He continued, "I wanted to forget my past in Auschwitz because I didn't want it to affect my future with Luiza but for the Nazi's and collaborators, a twisted reality formed the basis of their reasoning to forget. I find it repulsive they can even contemplate it, after what they'd done. I was concealing my life as a prisoner before Aleksy liberated me, I thought the Holocaust had damaged me beyond repair, but I found a way of surviving it all, my way. I didn't deny it, I just never spoke of it, but these people are inhuman. Like cowards, they hide from themselves and the reality of what they've done." He paused then pointed at the file.

"It was a trial unlike any other before, forty-five people all under the same process, it must have been confusing. If you think what we're doing now is complicated, then take a read of the Belsen trial notes." A sigh escaped him as he shook his head slowly. "I can't help but wonder how those people made sense of it all; the thousands of testimonies and notes within each of the trials. We've had years to prepare ourselves, we have prior knowledge, *they* were thrown into an abyss."

He told me of the 'crossovers' within cases and warned me I had to be conscious of the work I was doing and not be tempted to follow a lead that would walk me down another path. It was so easy to do, he said, but following it would take you to yet another one down the line and you'd end up going round in circles with the pure mass of information. "My advice is to stick to your task and don't go off on a tangent," he informed me.

Aleksy had said the same thing to him, there was just too much work involved, the overall picture couldn't ever be achieved if we didn't stick to the rules. It's picking away at justice, taking a little piece of it at a time, an SS guard here, a Kapo there, it's the only way to achieve some kind of solution. Aleksy called it, '*The Continuous Solution.*'

"I've spent days reading the Belsen trial notes, trying to make some sense to it all, there are so many names to try and link in ways I don't yet know how to," Emil told me. "Eugene, this is where you come in, if you want the job that is," he said.

"I'd be proud to take it on," I replied, and he smiled in return. At that point I realised my life would change, I'd no longer work on tedious cases for the NYPD, things would be interesting in the years ahead of me and I knew it at that very first meeting with Emil Janowitz, my new boss.

As we settled after the formal interview, Luiza offered some lunch, so laid back was the situation I stayed for the afternoon, listening to the rest of Emil's life story, which was fascinating. I told him he should write a book.

He'd received a letter recently, quite out of the blue, from an old friend, a man called Lars Kowalski. They'd not been in touch for nearly forty-five years. He told me, "It took a little while for it to sink in. He'd seen my name in a news report about the Kapo trials and decided to seek me out. After an exchange of letters, he called me on the telephone and let me know he was well, which pleased me." They'd last seen each other back in 1949 when Emil left Przemysl trying to find a new life for himself. They'd been best friends after the war. "I spoke to him on the telephone, can you imagine, nearly fifty years have passed since we'd last had a conversation and he was exactly as I remembered him." A big smile spread across his face, you could tell Lars had been an important person in his life, someone who'd touched his heart. I could see Emil was a good man, someone I'd become friends with, not just a work colleague.

"You still have friends from the old days, Emil, that's wonderful," I said.

He replied, "In those days, keeping in touch with people was a lot different than it is today, although that's somewhat of an excuse, I could have mailed a letter, I suppose, but I wrapped myself up in my new life, and hadn't wanted Luiza to find out my past. I just thought it best all around." He wasn't sad when he said this; to the contrary, his enthusiasm bubbled as he continued, "Lars' time in Bełżec extermination camp mirrored my own in Auschwitz, our friendship was born from a fight for life, we endured the same tortures and bore witness to the same atrocities. I'm pleased to hear from him, not only is he alive, but he's coming to visit," he said with great pleasure. "After all this time my friend had survived, our defiance in the face of the Nazis had won, they didn't destroy us." A weak smile and then he changed the mood.

"Getting back to the job, Quinn somehow talked Ilse Gerver into some kind of interview situation, feeding into her ego with a tale of a documentary programme. He's a particularly good liar, I like that about him. What are your interviewing skills like, Eugene?" he asked.

"I've a good track record, Emil. I like taking the bull by the horns, but I know when not to ask questions and just placate the witness, lulling them into a false sense of security," I replied.

"That's good Eugene, you're going to need all of those skills," he said. That's when I knew I'd definitely got the job. I stood and shook his hand. My first interview in twenty years had gone well. Emil gave me a copy of the Ilse Gerver file, telling me to study it in depth then passed me a copy of the Belsen files headed 'Law Reports of Trials of War Criminals' and said to try to extract some information from it that would assist us in our investigations.

The next day back at the flat, I tried to go through the 158 pages of trial notes. I read the crimes presented against Gerver and could see the verdict was guilty, some of her colleagues were given the death sentence but the crucial evidence against her failed to materialise; exhibits were missing, and several witnesses failed to turn up. She'd slipped the noose along with one other.

I met up with Findlay Quinn over a beer to get acquainted; we compared notes for the forthcoming meeting with Gerver, sharing our interview techniques, fine-tuning how we'd play this thing out. Quinn had worked on her for weeks whilst posing as a sympathiser, telling her he and his colleagues wanted to counterbalance the untruths that had been told. We'd play to her ego, allow her to become comfortable with us both, then we'd lead her into her crimes.

He and I clicked straight away, I felt at ease in his company and that was important to me, I knew we'd work well together. 'Fin', as he liked to be called, would take the lead with questioning, he'd spent months gaining her trust, using the skills he'd nurtured over the many years as a cop in the Bronx.

We flew out of JFK on Friday, the 12th of March 1995. It would be a long flight; we'd land the following day at

Rostock, Germany, our destination the small town of Teterow where Ilse Gerver lived.

Quinn seemed a little agitated on the journey; I think he was a nervous flyer, which I thought surprising for an ex-Navy Seal. We stayed in the Hotel Blucher in the city centre, planning to visit Gerver the following day. On arrival, we made use of the bar and settled easily into our stay after the long flight.

The next morning, in response to our knock, we were greeted at the front door by an aged woman whose height and lower protruding jaw line stood out as a feature; earlier photographs and some old film footage showed the same characteristic. Her hair was bedraggled and she had dark piercing eyes that seemed to penetrate right through you; for a woman of her age, she still looked formidable.

She invited us into the living room and I positioned the camera we'd brought along and attached a microphone to her lapel. She settled into a chair with a cup of tea Fin had made whilst I was setting up.

Fin started the interview. "Hello, Ilse, firstly, can you tell me a little about yourself?"

"Yes, I was born here in Teterow in 1921. I had quite a normal childhood, although I was called names a lot because of my looks, you know children say such things, 'daddy long legs' or 'bucket jaw'. They are so cruel," she said, reaching out for sympathy.

"I was in the 'League of German Girls' in 1939 and had also trained as a nurse. In 1942, I joined Ravensbruck Camp as a guard, *this was a mistake*," she said, suggesting an excuse.

"How did you get the job in Ravensbruck, Ilse," I asked.

"I was conscripted, *I didn't volunteer*. I was trained as a guard for four weeks," she said, starting to open up to the questions presented to her.

In the beginning, we took it easy, building her trust in us up. I was adept at this kind of interviewing but we both knew we had some hard questions to ask and hoped that, now in her later years, she might want to get some of the crimes she'd committed off her chest. We skirted around the issues we really wanted to talk about and Ilse was happy to oblige.

At 73, she was still an intimidating woman, a little shorter than her youthful six foot three and somewhat awkward in her manner but you could still sense an evil residing within her.

Fin finally said, showing her his file, "You served six of your ten years in prison, it says here, leniently allowed out early."

"Yes, that's true. But before that, they made me move the bodies of the rotting dead Jews that had typhoid. They refused us gloves, the arms and legs of those most rotted would just break off and, because they worked us all day, I injured my back and I have suffered from this ever since," she said with disgust. Unable to disguise her underlying hatred for the former inmates, she laid blame and sought pity.

Attempting to feign concern for her, I said, "Would you like a break Ilse, we've quite a lot to go through. Not all of the filming we'll do now will make it to the final cut; an hour's footage will be condensed down to maybe half an hour." It was all part of the strategy, lulling her into believing we were making a documentary about her life, hoping to portray the person inside the uniform and it seemed to be working. She wanted to be shown in a better light, I could feel it, but Fin and I had carefully planned the execution of this interview.

"So, at the Belsen trials, you were accused of sending people to Block 25 which was, I'm led to believe, selection for transport to Auschwitz and the gas chambers. What do you say to those who criticise you for doing that now, nearly fifty years after the war?" Fin asked, suddenly.

"Well, I was accused of a lot of things, but nothing ever stuck," she said with a twisted look on her face.

"We'll cut that, Gene, if you don't mind," Fin said to me, deliberately before continuing: "Now, Ilse, we all want to show you in a good light so whilst I know you want to answer, let's get some contrition in there," he said smiling at her, touching her hand with a comforting look on his face. Jesus, he was good, I thought, really good.

"Ilse, when you sent this particular group to Block 25, did you know they'd wait for two days for vans to pick them up to take them to the transports?" He left a small gap then said, "Ok, cut at this point Gene," then continued, smiling at her. "Ilse, what we'll do now is splice this thing together with our scripted answer. I've taken it upon myself to write a few lines, here take a look," he said passing a piece of paper over to her. She read it out loud, "No, I was unaware of the length of time they had to wait; I was just following SS orders."

As we'd planned, I simulated stopping the camera several times as we recorded whilst Fin drew out Ilse Gerver's confidence. In those supposed moments between takes, in the seemingly private conversation she had with Fin, she admitted to the cries of the children and knowing the prisoners would wait in torment; victims knowingly awaiting their deaths, no food and insufficient water.

The interview went perfectly. As the ex-guard smugly owned up to beating an 18-year-old Hungarian woman to death with a block of wood, unaware the camera was still rolling, her utter vileness was caught on film for all to see. Once she felt comfortable with 'people of her own kind', led on by our smiles and nods of agreement, it was difficult to stop her. We talked for roughly four hours and gained all the admissions we needed to back up the witnesses we'd found and could still find.

She was unapologetic for her crimes and proud of her nickname. "You know what they called me," she'd asked, with obvious delight. "They called me 'The Bitch of Belsen.' She pointed her finger at us as if playfully chastising a child. "This was because I was wise to them and wouldn't let them get away with idleness and lies."

Her age gave no excuse for her crimes, her belief in National Socialism still stood at the fore of her ideals and hatred ran through her like a virus.

We were talking, off-camera, about another female camp guard alleged to have had 34 prisoners hung during her time, and comparing it with Ilse's lesser infractions when she suddenly said, "Yes, wait a minute, it might be still there but you'll have to go up, my legs can't climb the ladder anymore."

"Sorry, Ilse, what do you mean?" I asked, thinking she was confused.

"The files, I placed my testimony in with the files, it will still be up there, in the loft," she said with a smile, getting up and beckoning us to follow.

As I entered an unpleasantly damp and cold attic, she told me the file would be in a corner, against a wall, in a satchel. It was obvious nobody had been up in it for many a year. I took a torch to see my way; it was pitch black apart from a small light breaking through the eves that lit up the far side of the huge space. After a few moments getting my bearings, I used the rafters to balance myself as I precariously stepped across on the beams and there in the corner, where she'd said it would be, was the satchel.

Strap still attached, I took it and threw it over my shoulder then retreated from the spider-infested misery, swiping furiously at the cobwebs now all over me. Ilse said, "Yes that's it, our little piece of security."

We went downstairs to reveal the contents. She told us she'd stolen some documents from Belsen before the liberation of the camp. Fin opened the buckles and pulled out a large file, within which were official-looking notes and documentation, swastikas and eagles stamped here and there. She'd kept it all hidden from the British Forces upon liberation.

I looked at Fin knowing she couldn't be allowed to keep such information, who knows what the contents would reveal, I thought.

He played the part. "Ilse, we're going to need to make copies of all these files for the documentary and your testimony will play a big part in it. This is fantastic, Ilse, these files may contain circumstantial evidence that may help exonerate you."

I cut in. "We can sign a receipt for you, get it photocopied and then send it back by secure courier, FedEx probably."

She suddenly became very angry and we caught a glimpse of the past in her. "No! No! No! I can't let you take them, they're all I have." She had a fearsome look on her face. I wasn't the only one taken aback.

I looked at Fin and said with emphasis and concern, "This could scupper the whole documentary and this stuff is probably crucial to it all. Jeez, the deadline is set and we need to get back to the states tomorrow, it's all booked. But what if something happened to the originals?"

Fin nodded, a serious look on his face. "I see where you're going there, Gene. If there was a break-in or maybe a fire then all this important documentation could be lost. I mean this could show the world that Ilse here was wrongly convicted. Hell, there'd probably even be some compensation money to be paid. If we hadn't committed ourselves to complete the other documentary it wouldn't be much of a problem, we'd just stay over the weekend and photocopy them at a post office or something. If we don't turn up for work on Monday it's going to cost us thousands, they'll sue our asses for breach of contract."

Ilse interrupted our purposeful conversation. "FedEx? So how long will that take," she asked, her mood switching from alarming one minute to a fairly pleasant old lady the next. I don't know what appealed to her more, the thought of vindication for her warped beliefs or the prospect of 'free' money. Fin gave her a reassuring smile. "You'll have it all back by Tuesday at the latest, I guarantee it, brought directly to the door by a secure courier."

We left Teterow that night with a videotape and some files that could possibly condemn Gerver and others to jail in their twilight years.

The flight back had Quinn unnerved again and we were met at the airport by Emil who was keen to find out how things had gone. We filled him in and he dropped me off at The Flat Iron building. I slept well that night and was feeling, for the first time in many years, that I'd done something enjoyable and worthwhile. Fin and I achieved what we'd set out to do.

The next morning, Emil phoned, dragging me from my sleep. "Have you looked at this file," he said enthusiastically.

"Not in detail, Emil, we didn't have that much time to get to the airport after the interview."

"It's dynamite," he said, like a young boy enthused by a new toy at Christmas.

"Are you coming in today?" he said half-jokingly.

I looked at the clock, stifling a yawn. "Yes, I'll be down this afternoon, I didn't get in until late." Then it dawned on me, "But you know that! You dropped me off," I exclaimed.

He laughed. "Listen, take your time I'm just pulling your leg, you've done well, both of you. I've only just started reading the file and it names SS guards I can cross-reference with Aleksy's files. I'm sure I've read a name somewhere at some point," he said. I could hear him thinking out loud, "Now, where was that file." He'd forgotten he was talking to me and had wandered off somewhere. I could hear papers shuffling and Luiza coming in the front door and then: "Jesus, sorry I do this all the time, are you still there," he asked."

"Yeah. Look, I'll jump the noon train and be at the house shortly after." "Sure, take your time," Emil said absently, other things on his mind. "You did well Eugene, you did very well."

As I lay in bed, musing on the job I'd found, one that filled me with enthusiasm and belief, I saw the note Jody had left on the nightstand before going to do her night shift. Too tired when I got home, I'd not noticed it before.

'Missed you, see you later, hope the job's gone well.' It was signed off with two kisses.

Like slowly drying wet footprints left on a bathroom floor, the Nazis thought that time would make things go away. Ilse Gerver had also but she was very much mistaken.

Chapter 2
The Belsen Files

I arrived in Greenwich on time and walked to Idar Court. An excitement I'd not felt in a long time gripped me, the thought of what Emil had told me earlier was electrifying. Luiza greeted me at the front door and showed me through to the study. I noticed the plaque above the doorway reading 'Harry' and I smiled. He stood at the window unaware I'd walked in. "Hello, Emil," I greeted him.

"Oh, Jesus Christ, I didn't hear you come in," he said, as papers dropped from his hands to the floor in response to my unannounced entrance.

"Hello, Eugene, I was in a world of my own. Did you get some rest after the flight?"

"Yes, I'm fine, what have you found, Emil," I asked, enthusiastically.

"The file you gave me, it's quite extensive, Ilse Gerver stole this for a reason Eugene, and that was to save her sorry little *ass*, and from what I've read so far, it names specific SS men. Her intention was clearly to use the information to fend off the hangman's noose if called upon. It details the duties and responsibilities within Belsen Concentration Camp and the actions within, for instance here," he pointed at a line on a sheet of paper, headed 'Bestrafungsregister'. "This is only one of several sheets listing beatings and other punishments officially recorded and it shows who carried out the work". He paused.

"I'm working on a name, Hans Schröder," he announced. "Somehow, I know this name, it jumped out of a page at me but I can't find it again. I've read it or seen it somewhere before. I've read thousands of transcripts over the years, but this was different, the hairs on the back of my neck stood up and I'm not sure why." He paused. "I want to utilise the computer Luiza bought, maybe create a spreadsheet, we can access names and events much more efficiently. It'll take up a hell of a lot of time but I think it'll be worth the effort."

As none of us were computer experts, I suggested, "Why don't we employ an agency and price the job up, we could have full access to the files within a week or so."

"Now why didn't I think of that? That's a damn good idea, Eugene. Do you think it's possible we could do that so quickly?"

"Leave it with me, I'll go into town and look around," I replied.

He smiled, conspiratorially. "I'll take a walk with you; it'll do my legs the world of good. I need to get some fresh air in these old lungs and get out of this office for a while, we can maybe have a beer," he said, quietly under his breath, putting a finger to his lips so Luiza didn't hear.

We strolled into Greenwich and came across 'Able Office Services,' who upon request gave us an hourly rate to compile a database from the files, suggesting we buy particular software.

We were given a rough time scale and Emil mentioned, "I need you to give me a call if you come across a name in the files, it's really important, can you let the staff know to look out for it? It's 'Hans Schröder'. Also, if I gave you a sequence of words, could you ring me if it turns up?"

I told them I'd bring copies in later that afternoon and, after a few beers, Emil and I returned to Idar Court where he had a printer and photocopier in the garage which had never been set up, so we spent the afternoon doing just that, scanning the first set of files. When the last page printed off, I dropped the lot back at 'AOS' to get them started on the job.

For the next few weeks, I photocopied what seemed like thousands of pieces of Aleksy's files, which Emil had named, 'The Sikora Files,' after the little bird he'd told me about. I also spent a lot of time running back and forth between his office and the stationary shop for ink. We copied so many pieces of paper the printer gave up on us and we had to buy another. With roughly a thousand sheets remaining, the agency rang with news, something had turned up.

"Twenty-Three Latvian Jews, Mr Janowitz," I heard said over the phone, a pretty unique sentence someone had come across.

As Quinn had been working in the office on the Gerver case, ensuring that the authorities had adequate evidence to prosecute and would arrest her, all three of us went down to the store.

There it was, written on the screen in front of our eyes, they'd found that Gerver's Belsen files contained the duties of the SS officers quite precisely and Schröder's name was mentioned, although the context wasn't entirely clear at that time. However, in the Sikora files, they'd found his name alongside a date and time as being present at the hanging of 'Twenty-Three Latvian Jews.'

He was now a target for us, one of probably many but seeing as we still had a lot of photocopying to do it went on the back burner.

Eventually, the Agency finished the work and did a great job but it wasn't cheap. Added to that, we decided it best that we buy another computer just for the database which 'AOS' loaded for us. Emil didn't look too happy about paying out for the best available but Luiza reminded him he was still good for the money.

He'd been right, his hunch had paid off, by cross-referencing the files things were starting to come together. Aleksy's files had, through the many years of research, identified 'incidents' he'd put to one side under the heading 'Unsolved Crimes of the SS'. Ilse Gerver had unwittingly offered a name for one of them. We were pleased with the finding but knew it was only the first step. If Schröder was still alive he'd now be in his eighties and still living somewhere in South America. We had something to focus on. It was just too coincidental; it had to be the same person.

The one clear thing was, in Gerver's files, we had a source that could give us untold information and direction.

Over the next weeks, we worked on collating information about Schröder. He was known as a man with a terrible temper towards his subordinates and not afraid to show his violent side to his officers. He appeared to have moved from camp to camp within a space of 18 months or so. At the end of the war, he'd escaped via the 'Ratlines' turning up in Paraguay and then, some years later, Brazil. Within the files, we found further crimes where he'd been present, different camps, weeks apart. The evidence was stacking up and we knew it had to be the same individual.

Something within the files caught my eye one day. I called Emil over who was working alone on something. "Look, these are internal SS documents from Belsen, it shows here," I pointed at a piece of paper with orders signed by Adolf Haas, the Camp Commandant. It referred to the receipt of a Führerbefehl stating 'the contents of which are expressly forbidden to replicate' and went on to instruct all the staff of the camp to comply fully with the orders of Standartenführer Schröder. It was stamped and dated 'May 1944'.

Emil stood back from the table, he looked disturbed. "Schröder moves in high circles it seems."

"There's more, Emil," I said. "We've been going through everything where Schröder's mentioned, the database is fantastic for this sort of stuff. Fin discovered that every time his name came up at a camp the killing of Jews increased. At Majdanek, for instance, shortly after he arrived they began Aktion Erntefest. It means..."

Emil interrupted. "I know what it means, Eugene. Operation Harvest Festival." He shook his head in disgust. "Only the Nazis could have thought that up."

I continued. "Basically, over the next few months, they cleared the camp of all their Jews, including the sub-camps, Budzyn, Trawniki, Poniatowa, Krasnik, and Pulawy. By the end of March '44, even after accepting another 18,000, they had only 71 Jews left in a live population of just over 6,000 prisoners. Gassings and shootings, they weren't fussy. In the meantime,

Schröder had moved on to other camps, turning up in Belsen in May '44. Directly after that, they started to increase the transports of Jews out of Belsen to the extermination camps. Before, it looks like it had been a bit erratic but as they started to receive more due to rerouted transports there seems to have been a newfound 'will' to clear the camp, but only of Jews."

Emil muttered, "The Final Order?" Fin and I looked at him questioningly. He gave us a sad wisp of a smile. "There's something in my files. I dimly recall an intelligence report, the interrogation of a German camp guard. No doubt trying to curry favour, he mentioned seeing a Hitler Order on his commandant's desk when he took something in for his attention. His boss was discussing something with a Standartenführer the SS man hadn't seen before. As I recall, the guard called it 'The Final Order'. Of course, he was questioned at length but all I can remember that he said in answer was that he hadn't seen a signature."

He saw our somewhat curious faces and went on. "He'd said it was a Hitler Order but it wasn't signed. They asked him how he knew and he told them it had 'Adolf Hitler' typed on the bottom." As further explanation, he offered, "The Allied Intelligence had been looking for definitive proof that Hitler issued such an order. I was going to follow it up but time and other things got in the way."

I asked, "Can you remember if he told them anything it said?"

"Oh, yes, Emil answered, absently. *"Destroy the remaining Jews of Europe."*

I looked at Fin. "Then let's see just how good this new system is," he grinned. I nodded back, swung myself into the seat and began tapping away.

Now with two assistants working under him, Emil had thought Luiza would go back to her normal life but, at her insistence, she helped out with our research. One of the things we discovered was information that showed, as the Soviets advanced, the SS had been given orders to burn all camp documentation, destroy the crematoria and gas chambers and take all those still alive with them as they fled towards the West. Not wanting to fall into Communist hands, they left the sick behind and shot anyone who was slowing them down along the way. In their haste to leave, not all the evidence was destroyed completely. Yet, by pure chance, we'd come across the

Belsen Files in Ilse Gerver's loft, files that would no doubt have been burnt if not for Gerver's need to escape the noose yet somehow she'd smuggled them out.

Yeah, sure, I knew about some of this stuff before but not the full extent and as I read extensively about the factories of death and how they were run, my disgust was overpowering. I'd later get 'used' to the atrocities because I had to become cold about the case files, somehow putting the crimes aside in a box in my head labelled 'History,' convincing myself that by doing so it would make the victims not seem so real. It was something I'd done subconsciously in Homicide and upon realising it I'd had to accept my decision.

Our database took us to the relevant papers in the Sikora files and, after confirming what Emil remembered, we set about trying to trace the guard in question. The intelligence people, on being told there was no Hitler signature on the document seen, had soon tired of being nice to him and pressured him in respect of his involvement in camp activities. It seems he wasn't just involved in the 'Admin Office. At the trials, he got 5 years, served 3 and was deported to his home town, then in communist East Germany. That's where the trail went stone cold and all we had was his original story, but it made us think.

The Standartenführer he'd seen in discussion with his Camp Commandant over the 'The Final Order' document had to be Schröder, we all agreed on that, but why no signature? The Allies had captured previously written Hitler Orders; the infamous T4 euthanasia order that authorised the killing of those considered to be 'feeble minded' and a drain on the Nazi state. There was also the Commando order which decreed that such soldiers were to be annihilated and were not to be allowed to surrender. His signature was clearly on these documents. We discussed it at length, especially after we found a detailed record of Schröder's late SS service. He'd been their liaison officer to Albert Speer, the Minister for Armaments and War Production and a temporary liaison between Himmler and the Fuehrer's HQ, but the most interesting thing was his posting to 'Amt IV B' of the infamous Reich Security Main Offices. The innocuously titled 'department IV-B-4-c Evacuations' was the administration offices for 'Sonderaktion 1005'; the operation carried out after the 'Aktion Reinhard' killing spree to cover up the slaughter. Bełżec , Sobibor, Treblinka and Majdanek were names Schröder would have known well. His later presence at the major killing centres just before significantly increased activity with a document purporting to be a direct order from Hitler couldn't be ignored.

Emil voiced it before we were able to. "You know, there are people on the internet who claim Hitler never signed such an order. What if that's the only thing they are right about? What if the ardent and totally committed Nazi, Schröder, recognised the current military situation, far better than the deluded Hitler, and was savvy enough to know that presenting his Führer with a proposal to hurriedly speed up the destruction of Europe's Jews was almost an admission of defeat and one that could only result in him standing in front of a bullet-ridden wall somewhere." He paused to let it sink in. "But, I think, he saw an opportunity to put the plan into play by faking a Fueherbefehl. He'd worked at Hitler's headquarters; he knew how things got done. He knew how to make things work. What if Schröder wrote Hitler's instruction?"

I had to agree it was very much possible and Fin added, "But, I reckon, even *he* hadn't realised the situation on the Eastern front would escalate so quickly which probably accounts for his frantic activity as the months wore on."

It was a reasonable conclusion, Hans Schröder was the real author of 'The Final Order'.

FedEx finally delivered the box from The Simon Wiesenthal Centre, we eagerly read through its contents, sat around Emil's study passing sheets between the three of us, trying to extract some information that could assist us regarding the whereabouts of the Standartenführer, reading and re-reading in case we'd missed something, some small detail, a word or a phrase that could trigger the answer we so wished for.

We found nothing, Schröder's last known sighting was in São Paulo, Brazil, his existence after 1973 unknown. He'd disappeared, possibly dead. Were we chasing a ghost? We had our doubts at that stage, we thought it was a lost cause. Quinn said as much, but Emil didn't give up, he kept us going with his appetite for justice. He said, "If he's dead so be it, but his crimes would not stay unsolved, we go on with the job to prove he gave The Final Order." The fire in his belly rubbed off on us both. We agreed with what he'd suggested, realising it would be a battle to get any further. We did get one thing though, Emil found a small envelope inside a pocket of the Wiesenthal Schröder file, within were photocopies of his fingerprints and a 'Führer Ausweis': SS identity card with his photograph. The photo looked like it was taken around the time he would have visited Belsen. Taken in dress uniform, white shirt, black tie, peaked cap, death's head badge with the Eagles wings above, it was in remarkably good condition considering its age. The fingerprints were in a thin protective sleeve and the originals from which they'd been copied had been a little smudged, which you'd expect from prints of that age.

Fin decided he'd use some of his South American special forces contacts, people he'd trained or actively worked with who he knew could be trusted but even they came up with nothing.

Alternatively, I suggested I should concentrate my efforts on making use of the computer; I'd use search engines to attempt to find names, addresses, national insurance numbers. In the Sikora files, I pulled out all I found that could be cross-referenced with the Schröder case, hoping something would just talk to me.

I kept everything together on 'floppy disks' so I could work from home. I thought being under each other's feet all day was unhealthy for a working environment. I also knew I could bury myself within the files in a lot more in-depth without interruption, Jody always kept herself to herself when I was working, offering a sandwich and tea when needed, but wouldn't interfere with my working hours. If I needed something from the database, I'd call Luiza and she'd sort it for me. It saved on travel and I got to spend more time with Jody.

I worked on Schröder's files for nearly two weeks, searching his name, via birth, marriage and death records, and at some point, I realised I was going around in circles and that was the one thing I'd been instructed not to do. I had to come at this another way, I thought. I started thinking like Schröder would and phoned Emil to bounce ideas off him, the way cops do, attempting to find something, anything. It was Emil who got there first, "Think about it, Eugene, he was a high ranking SS officer. I'm quite sure he didn't make all these visits solo. He probably had a driver or bodyguard," he said thinking out loud, and then the light bulb moment, "We're looking in the wrong place, Eugene," he said. "Go on," I encouraged, not entirely sure where he was going. "We're searching in the darkness when we should be looking for the light," he said. Then it came to me also. "Jesus, you're right! We need to look for his 'shadow', if we find him maybe we find the man," I said. It was clear, I needed to research Schröder's closest contacts during his period of frantic activity. Sure, he could have just used a driver from the SS motor pool but these were long journeys, overnight stays on the way. He'd have wanted a 'fellow traveller', someone who understood the issue and the urgency, someone he got along with. I needed to look for a 'best pal.'

Quinn, meanwhile, received bad news regarding the Gerver case. She'd never face trial. Ilse took her own life. She was found with a short rope tied around her neck and the stair bannister; she'd ended her life in the same manner she'd taken others. There was a sort of justice in it though. We speculated whether she'd noticed we'd sent her back copies of the Belsen files and kept the originals. If she had, she'd probably realised what was coming next, an exposé and a trial. Too much to bear it seemed. Fin's contacts in the German prosecutor's office told him she'd burnt a pile of documents in the days before the final act.

Otto Weiss was a decorated SS Untersturmführer who'd risen from the ranks and, I discovered, he'd first served with Schröder during the early years. He was the only one of his associates that kept turning up in the same places at the same time. My last find, the one that clinched it, was an Amt IV B personnel list from late '43. I cross-referenced him with the Sikora files and found seven occurrences of them together in one form or another. It all took place fifty years ago and a lot of the information we were working on was hearsay, but seven occurrences made me sit up and pay attention even more. Trawling through what would have taken months of research just a few weeks back, it'd only taken a matter of days with my head buried deep within the files.

There were some things I just couldn't do from home. When Luiza told me she'd found amongst the many box files they'd inherited from Alexsy one with Weiss's name on it, I had to rush into Idar Court to pick it up.

Working through it, I came across a book that seemed to be in the wrong place at the wrong time. I wondered who'd put it there and why. I opened up the pages and read the words, "Love and warmth were missing in my household as a child," words written some years back, the book had been burnt and some pages were torn, it was an autobiography. The words written, you'd have thought, should have encouraged some sympathy within you, but these words were written by a man synonymous for being the right-hand man and confidant of Adolf Hitler.

I considered the book and wondered why it was in Otto Weiss's file notes, it confused me somewhat. Albert Speer had escaped the hangman's noose at the 'Nuremberg Trials,' a highly intelligent man who didn't possess the one thing that condemned his fellow war criminals: *arrogance*. His intellect and appearance of honesty had saved his life. He gave the prosecution what they wanted to hear and fell upon his own sword, accepting guilt, condemning himself for *apparently* not knowing the atrocities that had taken place. By doing so, he fed into the lie, a lie that would paint him as the Good Nazi.

I considered the book but put it to one side, maybe it would become of use at some point in my investigations. There had to be a reason such a high-profile Nazi's book had been placed within a file of the man I was now researching but because of its age and somewhat delicate nature, I later found a copy in the history section of a book store in Greenwich and bought it, promising myself I'd find the time to read it at night.

I believed Otto Weiss would be pivotal to our investigation so I focussed all my attention on him and hoped he was still alive.

I scoured the internet for his name, finding several namesakes in Brazil, narrowing them down little by little. I was looking at births, deaths and marriage records, driving licences, insurance, community records and being an ex-cop, I pulled in some favours and utilised criminal records databases which came back with a name, address and age. It was the only one out of the seven records that fitted all the parameters, it was either this or we'd have to try Paraguay, I thought.

I looked closely at a company I'd found in the overseas registries of companies, one named 'Forge Ore', Otto Weiss was the CEO, along with six directors, Lars Hencke, Peter Wächtler, Philipp Heinig, Max Von Weber, Josef Rösler and Janik Schön. They would all need scrutinising, maybe something in their past would hand this particular Otto Weiss on a plate to me. Yeah, I was looking for a needle in a haystack, but that's what I was good at, I had a nose for coincidence and followed it through until I got a conclusion. I scrutinised their names, they were all German.

I considered the odds of that, seven directors working in Brazil together, it was one of the things that stuck in my mind, the detective in me asking questions constantly, and the word 'Forge' was saying something to me. I read the company's website and got to know what they were about, yet something was gnawing away at me, I'd come back to it, I thought, making a post-it note and placing it upon my screen.

It was something I did regularly, discarding them when the problem was resolved or irrelevant to the case anymore, it may end up as another note thrown in the bin for all I knew, but I'd return to it when ready, or more likely when my brain found the time and space. I gave regular updates to both Emil and Fin, remembering I was still on the payroll and had to earn my wage. I ordered some FORGE company statements and paid the fee involved; I wasn't sure if any information would turn up in the interims or full-year reports, but the hunch I'd had was playing with my mind, and my gut instinct hadn't let me down in the past. Emil was encouraging, he knew when a cop had something bugging him, he'd had that feeling too, "Go with it Eugene, see how far you can get," he'd offered up.

I started with Lars Hencke, a director of the company from its inauguration; a seventy-nine-year-old man, who, from my research had no past before 1973, just like Weiss. The formation of Forge had put him on the map, one I could now read. I thought it strange though, or too coincidental. I quickly moved onto the other directors and found similar patterns, some appeared in the mid-sixties' others didn't seem to exist at all before 1960, it looked to me like they'd planned the formation of the company a long time before, all unifying when Otto Weiss appeared on the scene, it was like they were waiting for him. Maybe he had the finances for the project, I thought. I was stretching without facts and I knew that was a dangerous road to go down, so I slowed up a little.

I pulled out information from the reports I'd ordered, stock worth, market cap etc, the company had done well or so it seemed, mainly dealing in iron ore but also dabbling in precious metals as a by-product, yet I couldn't find any proof of volumes for that, Exporting to China, they had a limitless order book for ore, each Director a share holder of the company and all multi-millionaires, the shares were trading at $1.12 on the AMEX, and looking back over a period of five years, the share price had risen from twelve cents, quite a significant investment for the seven shareholders. I knew there was something I was missing, it was like someone whispering in your ear, something you just can't hear and out of range, it was annoying. I had to establish the Otto Weiss I was looking for was the same one I was investigating at FORGE, and find a way of doing that. Talking with Emil had given me the insight, "Look back into the files we have, run the names, you never know what might turn up," He'd encouraged. I did just that and Emil was right again, I found Janik Schön within the Sikora Files, he'd been SS at Belsen, it was all I needed to give the green light to my suspicions, I was on the right track.

I was frantically researching into Forge Ore, wanting to find a link to Hans Schröder, he'd be at the top of the chain if still alive, or so I thought. So many Nazis had escaped via the rat runs to places like Brazil, Paraguay and Argentina, he'd have been one of them, I was sure of that and wanted him for Emil's sake, I knew how much it meant to him. Schröder was high up in command, high enough to get close to 'The Führer' himself. Was it possible after all these years we'd stumbled upon the man who gave the final order? Ilse Gerver's files had given us the possibility of doing just that, I had to pinch myself at the thought of it, I'd been working for Emil for just a matter of months, and this was now at the top of the pile of paperwork sitting on my desk.

I didn't get carried away though, experience had taught me that, just when you think you've got it in the bag, you'd hit a brick wall.

Emil phoned, he'd been intrigued by my findings, so much so he'd taken some time out at the weekend to do a little digging himself, which was the reason for the call. "I've got six guys with differing entry points into Brazil, whose aliases are unknown prior to entry, yet we can assume they had something to do with Otto Weiss and Belsen before they entered Brazil, so I took it upon myself to do a little delving into the past of the other six. I've gotten quite used to this computer now and find it really helpful with research. I didn't mean to but I found myself on a website that had a column by a British author, a well-known Holocaust denier. It kind of drew me in, and with the knowledge we've uncovered, I had to take a look. You see, he denies the order was ever given by Hitler, in fact, in his own words, he says, "Hitler had neither ordered the extermination of the Jews nor had known about the Holocaust," he said, his disdain apparent "He even denies the Holocaust ever happened! I'd like to talk to that man and explain my whereabouts between the years of 1943 and 45, and tell him what happened to my family. I find this man ignorant and repulsive Eugene," he said with a mix of anger and sorrow.

I tried calming him. "Emil, allow me to do this, it's your day off remember, Luiza's earned your company on a Sunday, spend some time with her, and don't go upsetting yourself over some damn fool on the Internet." "No, sorry Eugene, that's not why I called you. I've been distracted by *that* man. What I meant to tell you is that whilst I was going through the search engine, I don't know how, but pages kept popping up on me. I must have clicked on something or other, anyway Luiza says we have a virus on the computer, she's trying to sort it out at the moment, but one of the pages that came up was another Holocaust denial page and one of its pictures intrigued me, so I printed it off before the computer crashed." He paused for some time. As he often did, Emil had walked away from the phone again, a trait of his I'd gotten used to quite quickly.

"Emil!" I shouted down the line. "Yes, I'm sorry, I was giving Luiza my cup and forgot what I was doing, I do it all the time, it's an age thing, "he told me. "Yes, Emil, that's alright, but the photograph you printed off," I asked.

"Yes. It was Josef Rösler, it actually named him," he said.

I told him I'd come in the next day to see the photograph, "Maybe we can re-find the website you found the photograph on," I told him.

For the remainder of that day, I read through files on the computer, delving into Rösler's life as deep as I could, trying to put together a story, a pattern of events that would have brought these seven men together within Brazil. I questioned myself many times, it's a line of investigation I go down to get answers, sometimes a wrong question can throw up a right answer and that answer can give you the right question. You had to look at things a little skewed to find the real question you should be asking.

Emil had been helpful, why was Josef Rösler on a Holocaust denial website? I'd found my question, now I needed the answer. I'd been researching Forge Ore until Emil's phone call; I hadn't found what I was looking for. I still couldn't find records showing quantities of produce mined other than iron ore and it intrigued me, why could I find the ore with ease and not the precious metals, was it business etiquette? I was researching things I knew little about but I couldn't see a reason why it wouldn't be readily available to shareholders.

Maybe that was it, I'd have to buy shares in the company to get the full reports I thought so I sent a question to a broker friend of mine; he had an office in Jackson Heights. He emailed me back an answer. "It's possible, Gene, but highly unlikely I'd say, most businesses have to be crystal clear with their filings, any information should be readily available unless it's detrimental or misleading to the share price," he'd said. "Buy a few shares, you never know, good luck with it, Geno," the message ended. After talking to Emil, my thought process had changed somewhat and as I ran through what I was doing before his call, sitting back in the chair refreshing my mind, it struck me, maybe that was the point. I couldn't find quantities of by-products because there weren't any. I made a post-it note and stuck it onto my screen.

Otto Weiss and Hans Schröder were on our radar, I knew we'd found something. Instinct was telling me to continue down this road and it would come good. Fin had been working on another line of investigation and he filled me in. Something was going on between Ilse Gerver and Rudi Baumann, a guard at Belsen. Now dead, Gerver could give no insight to us but Fin wouldn't let that deter him, he was a tenacious guy. He wasn't giving up on her part in this and said, "The cards are all starting to stack up, Gene, the only thing that's stopping us now is time and, at the moment, we've got plenty of that on our side."

Chapter 3

Night and Fog

I told Emil that Fin had found a relationship existed between Baumann and Gerver but, on the phone, he dismissed it as irrelevant. Personally, I believed it may have had some bearing on how she'd got hold of the files from Belsen in the first place. I thought it odd he hadn't considered it of interest, but then recalled his words not to go down blind alleyways, so I made a post-it note and placed it alongside many others.

I continued scrutinising Forge Ore and the coincidences presenting themselves to me, then, whilst I was researching something that had been playing on my mind, I came across the words, 'Bundesrepublik Deutschland'. I stared at the screen and it stared back at me for several moments whilst I contemplated exactly what it was I was looking at. Then it sank in. We called it the 'Federal Republic of Germany', the shortened version of which was 'FRG.' I knew immediately it was what had been bugging me.

The company name 'FORGE' contained the three letters FRG, not only that but if I expanded the idea,

'**Fe**deral **R**epublic **Of GE**rmany' was also jumbled into the name. I didn't quite know what it meant yet other than a possible hidden admission of where the origins of the company had been born but I'd got something and I knew it; I just needed to do some more digging.

Quinn phoned me later that night, "Emil's house has been turned over. They shot his dog for Christ's sake. Luiza rushed him to the vet's and he's in surgery as we speak, I think he'll survive, he's a tough old boy, but both Emil and Luiza are beside themselves with worry. Emil said he'd left some paperwork on his desk, papers from the Belsen Files which have been taken. Max had a note lying alongside him, it just said 'For Ilse'. Obviously, someone's found out what we're investigating."

"Jeez, Fin, who could possibly know?" I questioned, I was worried for Jody as I said the words.

"Nobody, all I submitted was some paperwork to get a court hearing, the courts hadn't even been informed of a date yet," Then he said, slowly, thinking out loud, "But I did let the Police Department know my intentions. Leave it with me, Eugene. You go over and spend a little time with them, see they're alright, and don't let

Daniel and Lena know about Max, they wouldn't want that."

Emil's children had only recently found out about his past and, from what Fin had told me, they weren't best pleased about him coming out of retirement. It would be too much to explain at this precise moment. Quinn asked me to meet up with him later to run through some ideas. He'd a theory he wanted to run by me, get some foundation to what we were doing here. I agreed and said I'd meet up with him at 'Macduff's Bar' in Greenwich. I was thinking the same thing myself in fairness. Just as I was about to hang up, I remembered something. "Just a minute, Fin, if we're lucky, you know we haven't lost a god damn thing," I told him.

"Kennedy, we've lost a large part of the Belsen Files and god only knows what information that held, you couldn't paint a worse picture," he responded with not too fine a tone, emphasised I thought by calling me by my surname.

"No, no, remember the agency had a copy of everything, Fin. If they still have them we can get copies."

"Jesus, Gene, your right, sorry I was abrupt there, they've got nothing we can't replace then, apart from old Max, and maybe the knowledge we're onto them", he said and rung off.

As I arrived at Idar Court, a forensics van was parked outside, a young female officer bearing the name tag 'Darla Platt' was dusting a window for prints. She told me she might be able to lift a print from a pane of glass where the break-in had taken place and that she'd found a smear of blood on it as well as some blood on the floor inside, near to where Max had been shot and she was sure the first test had shown it to be human blood. I asked her, out of range of other officers, if she could run a match with the prints I had from the Wiesenthal Schröder file. I let her know how old the prints were and told her I had sound reasons to believe there was a possibility of a match. I used the old Kennedy charm and she reluctantly agreed. I left her to get on with her job whilst I tried to console Luiza who sat in the living room distressed. Max was on the operating table, fighting for his life, and they'd been sent home to await the outcome of the surgery.

Emil was making cups of tea and coffee for everyone, I could see he needed to keep himself busy to occupy his mind, his dog's situation weighed heavily on him.

Luiza tried telling me a little about Max. "He's such a good boy, and gentle you know, when he plays he never bites you hard, he wouldn't hurt you purposely, if by accident he does, he panics and licks you to make it all better. Eugene, why did they do this to Max? He doesn't do anybody any harm, he's just a dog, he's more likely to fetch you a ball than attack you if you broke into the house." She swallowed hard then wept uncontrollably. I held her close and kept my thoughts to myself, it wouldn't do anybody any good explaining the reason they'd shot Max, it would just make things worse. Luckily, Emil had wisely hidden the note from her.

I met up with Quinn later that night in the village. "Alright, here's what I've got so far, clearly somebody at the Police Department has let slip our operation. However, I can pay them a visit to ascertain who, where and why," Fin said whilst pulling out his notepad from his inside pocket. "This is how I see it so far, Ilsa Gerver was given the Belsen Files by the Nazi SS guard

Rudi Baumann. I think that's a safe bet, she'd have thought it was to protect her, I'm surmising he was looking after his own ass. She being a small cog in the big machine, she'd have been unimportant to him, the question I'm trying to work out is what Baumann was protecting himself against," he paused, looking at me for input.

It was a good question.

"It had to be something bigger, much bigger, but remember we don't want to walk down blind alleyways, Emil wouldn't want that," I cautioned. We sat drinking beer and talked over what solid evidence we actually had, ending the night agreeing to wander into Greenwich PD in the morning just to see if anyone had been making enquiries about Emil.

The next day, we walked into the foyer and approached the desk. To my surprise, I recognised the duty officer from my NYPD days. Antonio Kaufman was a heavy-set guy I'd played racket ball with, now and then, years back. They hadn't been kind to him, he'd put on more than a few pounds, likely due to the fact he was probably sat on his ass all day.

"Antonio, good to see you, what the hell are you doing here?"

"Eugene Kennedy! I could say the same thing." We shook hands as he continued, "I got tired of working the streets and found myself a sweet spot here. It's a bit more laid back, not a lot but enough to count. What *are* you doing here, by the way."

I introduced Fin and told him we were working the Janowitz case file. "He had his dog shot by an intruder," I added.

"Yeah, I heard about that one and that you were involved. How can I help you, Eugene?" he replied.

"Well, the thing is, it looks like a targeted attack. Fin and I believe the perp may have got his information from somewhere within these walls. Now, I'm not pointing any fingers here, Antonio, I'm just looking to find out if someone maybe called in or possibly asked for an address, something along those lines," I was cautious, not wanting to provoke a defensive attitude.

"You know what…" he hesitated whilst thinking. "A lawyer called in a few days back, said he worked for this ex-cop, Janowitz. I was at the desk. I knew him vaguely by sight from NYPD but asked him for his credentials and why he needed to know. He told me he'd left all Janowitz's contact details in his office and needed to fill out the paperwork for some court proceedings, something about Elsa, or was it Isla," he said, scratching his head.

"Ilse," I corrected him.

"Yeah, that's the name, anyway I ran a check on him and he checked out alright. His name's Leon Spiel, works out of Queens in a little office off Utopia Parkway. If you hang fire a minute I'll get you the address, I took it down," he said and walked off into the back office.

As he handed me the note, I asked, "Did you give him Janowitz's address?"

"Do you think I'm an idiot, Eugene?" He laughed then looked thoughtful. "Although, I did call to the guys in the back asking if they knew Janowitz and one of them called back that they thought he was still living in Hydra Court, I think it was."

"Idar Court, do you think, Antonio?"

"Yeah, that's it. Idar Court. But I never gave him the address. I told him we'd have to contact Janowitz first before we handed anything out. You know the drill,

Eugene. Anyway, he said he understood and would go back to his office and sort it out from there."

I gave him a sympathetic smile. "Were you standing next to Mr Spiel when you heard the guy in the back office say where Janowitz lived?"

The light bulb moment on Antonio's face was almost worth the journey. We bade each other a fond farewell, the word 'Buddy' falling meaninglessly from our lips.

As we walked away, he blustered, "Hey, he could have got it from the directory."

"He's un-listed, Antonio," I called back with a smile.

Knowing Emil hadn't instructed any such enquiry, Fin and I made an appointment over the phone with Spiel then headed on over to Queens without delay to pay a visit. Whilst Fin drove, I took a call from 'Able Office Services'. I'd called in a few days back and filled them in with what had happened and they'd obliged with my request for fresh copies of all the Belsen Files that were taken in the break-in. I asked if they could keep a master copy in storage, in case anything else happened, and for a small fee, they were happy to oblige, placing them into a safe store. At the time I wondered why we hadn't done that in the first place.

As we pulled up outside the Citibank at the junction of Union Turnpike, we saw an office above, signposted 'Leon Spiel, Lawyer LLM,' the guy we were looking for. We entered Spiel's office and were met by a squat balding man, a little Danny DeVito lookalike, the guy from the sitcom 'Taxi'.

"How can I help you, fellas?" he greeted us with an exaggerated Italian drawl, a little like he was serving at a bar in the Bronx.

I got straight to the point, "You made enquiries a few days back about a Mr Janowitz." Spiel nodded nervously, it was clear to see he was unsettled. Fin joined in the conversation, "Our client had his home ransacked and his dog shot two days ago, do you have anything you'd like to say about that?" he said, menace in his voice.

"Hey guys, I'm just a representative of the law myself here," he said, putting his hands out in front of him, palms towards us.

"Well, I'd say you've got some explaining to do, fella," Fin flatly stated and Spiel backed down a little.

"Look, I took a call from a guy called *Wise*, it was an easy cash job. All I had to do was find a name and a matching address. He said he was an old friend. With a name like *Wise,* I suppose I assumed he was Jewish."

Spiel was perspiring, worry was written all over his face, his little cash job could get him into some deep waters with the Law Society. Fin and I knew that, but it was something we could keep in our back pockets, an ace we could pull out, if and when needed. He hadn't done anything too outrageous and we knew that lawyers in New York pulled deals like it every day. Spiel hadn't intended to cause harm, he'd just been greedy and stupid, but we weren't prepared to let him off the hook that easy.

"How did you contact him? What's his number?" I asked.

"I don't have one. Honestly, guys, he called me." A bead of sweat trickled down the side of his face.

"How did he pay you? You said cash, so what does he look like?" I persisted.

"I never met him! I did the job. He called and said I should check my post box. The money was in a brown envelope."

Convenient, I thought. "You'll probably see us again. We may need to call on you for information but then again you may get lucky and we won't. Just sleep with one eye open from now on, Leon," I said whilst Fin gave Spiel a knowing glare, pointing a finger at his forehead, firing the non-existent pistol held in his hand. We turned and left.

That night I sat eating a meal with Jody in the apartment, mulling things over in my head, letting her know about Leon Spiel and his disposition, running through my thoughts about the man and what he'd told Fin and me. As I was telling her, I realised I was speaking with an accent without knowing I was doing it, offering her an interpretation of the way he spoke, then as I was saying the word '*Wise*', I stopped myself, "Hang on a minute, wise guy, wise!" My mind raced. Who were wise guys? The Mafia used the term, I'd read enough books and seen the films. Surely not? What could the Mafia want with Emil, it didn't make sense. I played with the words and sat for a while saying the word over and over in my head, then it struck me, "Jesus, I need to phone Fin", I exclaimed.

"Listen, Fin, the guy thought it was a Jew he spoke to on the telephone. Before I called you, I searched AOL, guess what turned up?" I left a deliberate pause.

"Go on," Fin countered, impatiently.

"The name Wise is an Americanised name formed from the German and Jewish dialect, it means 'White,' I told him.

"Gene, it's getting late, and I've got a hot meal sitting at the table, are you trying to make a point of some sort?" he said abruptly.

I had to be quick. "Ok, stay with me on this, just a minute of your time. Spiel believed his client was Jewish, he told us as much and said the name used was 'Wise'. In German, according to AOL, that translates as 'Weise'. I spelt it out. "Now that's some coincidence, or am I barking up the wrong tree here?" I asked. "There could be something," he replied.

"Ok, the spelling of the name is slightly different, but what's the chance of us looking for an Otto Weiss and a Mr 'Weise' shows up as connected to our crime scene?" I persisted.

"Yeah, but it still doesn't add up, Gene. Otto Weiss is German, our guy Spiel said the man on the phone was Jewish," he pointed out to me. "Now, how do you square that off?"

"You're right, Fin, but Spiel never mentioned the man on the telephone was *the* client. I need to think about this for a while, so go back to your meal and I'll talk with you in the morning," I said, putting the phone down.

There was something in this I thought, it was just too coincidental, for me anyway. Running it round and round my head, I sat with a coffee looking over Madison Square Park. I'd been lucky enough to get the option of a corner apartment which gave me a great view facing Broadway and the crowds of people below. I loved the apartment for that; it was an eye on the world. Over the years it had changed so much but it still retained its beauty. I sat contemplating my thoughts and, boy, you could really think looking out of that window. I tried to make some sense of what I'd just informed my partner and it wasn't coming easy but it *would*; after years on the force, I knew that much. I just had to encourage a little patience in myself, which wasn't such an effortless thing to do when I knew it'd keep me up nights.

The next day, I took a call from Darla Platt. "I've got the results from the break-in," she said. "I'm sorry to tell you but there's inconclusive evidence on the print but the blood on the glass came back AB negative. The implications of that aren't very helpful either I'm afraid, as far as I can see! You see the AB negative blood group is a rare blood type, the culprit had no match on our criminal records database and the fingerprints were negative. I think the case doesn't have legs to walk any further," she said.

"What about the other blood sample you took?"

"No, help there. I think I must have messed it up. It had two different DNAs in it so all I can think of is it got contaminated somehow. It's not usable."

I thought about mentioning the lawyer Spiel but something inside told me not to, so I thanked her for her time and phoned Fin. He was frustrated when I told him the news and suggested we pay Spiel another visit, see if we could 'encourage' him to remember something helpful.

Parking outside the office on Union Turnpike, we entered the front of the building and made our way to Spiel's office on the second floor. A receptionist sat at the front desk, she hadn't been there on our previous visit. Out of courtesy, we informed her of our intentions. "We're here to see Spiel," I said.

"I'm afraid Mr Spiel's not in his office at the moment. Can I take a message?" she replied. Fin told her not to worry; we'd give him a call.

"Good luck with that one, sir, I've been trying to get through to him for a while now," she replied, with a look of concern. I asked her about Spiel's reliability and habits.

"He's as reliable as you can get, it's just not like him," she replied. I thanked her for her help and we left.

Whilst Fin put some gas in the car at the Exon garage opposite, I wandered over the road to buy a couple of coffees at a place called 'Muscats'. I hadn't realised how hungry I was until I entered and I liked the look of the place so shouted over to Fin to follow on in. We sat talking over Spiel's absence and decided to take breakfast, both having the combo: two poached eggs on pita bread with feta cheese and black olives, drizzled over with olive oil. It filled a gap as we mulled over our next move. We realised we had to go back into Spiel's office; we couldn't afford to wait for him, that became clear to us both. I let Fin know I still retained my old

NYPD badge, I kept it in my inside jacket pocket. "You never know when it'll come in handy," I told him.

Returning to the receptionist, I briefly flashed the badge, informing her I'd been given permission to look over Spiel's office. I said I'd called the Precinct letting them know Spiel had gone absent and they'd instructed me to check his diary and anything that could ascertain his whereabouts. She didn't resist, which suited me just fine. Opening her desk drawer, she lifted out a mortice key on a piece of string and handed it over, saying, "You'll need to give the door a little push, it's quite stiff." Once inside, I closed the door behind Fin, turning the key in the lock. I didn't want prying eyes to see what we were up to.

Experience had taught us both where to look, searching through Spiel's records, database and Rolodex. We worked independently of one another, searching thoroughly for that elusive piece of detail that could open up the investigation to us. I found a bank statement, it was recent, I looked through it quickly and placed it into my inside jacket pocket. Fin found scribbled notes in Spiel's Filofax whilst I noted, "Most folk would carry that with them. Why would you leave your Filofax back in the office?"

A discarded post-it note found its way out of the bin and into my colleague's pocket. "I think we need to take that Rolodex Fin, it may shed some light," I said quietly and emptied the index cards into a bag he'd picked up at the Exon garage. We were in the office no longer than ten minutes, a thorough comb through and we unlocked the mortice and left, handing the key back to the receptionist on our way out, offering appreciation for her cooperation and bidding her farewell as she filed her nails.

We made the decision not to involve Emil at this point, thinking he needed a little time away from the job with his family but Fin took a call from him which sunk that idea. Emil was a tenacious guy, one you couldn't keep out the loop on anything. He asked how we were doing and requested our presence at Idar Court. He'd things to tell us he said, then added, "Oh and Max has pulled through the operation."

Whilst we both thought he was spending time with Luiza, he was actually working on the case. He said he'd uncovered things he didn't want talking about over the telephone so we agreed to meet him at a previously used rendezvous; he'd become very cautious since his dog had been shot. "There are eyes and ears everywhere gentlemen," he said, anxiety in his tone.

We met in the coffee house at the 'Bruce Museum,' not far from where Emil lived. Upon entering, he looked hesitant. "You know, this is where I met Aleksy Markowski," he said, looking out over Greenwich Harbour, obviously reminiscing about his old friend, and you could see a sadness coming over him. From what he'd told me, Aleksy had been a real special guy.

"Gentlemen, please sit down, I've been digging around into the company 'Forge Ore' and the connection to the FRG you mentioned a while back. You were right to be suspicious about their returns, Eugene," he said, with a smile beginning to emerge on his face. "I bought a few shares and had the updated interim reports sent through. Your suspicion was right, they don't appear to be mining any rare materials; nothing at all is evident. I asked a stock broker friend of mine to run over the reports for me and do a bit more digging. He said for all intents and purposes they're filing millions of dollars of sales in gold, silver and a number of other precious metals. He found that suspicious and told me they could be funnelling resources from elsewhere but the fact the reports showed nothing being disclosed in Brazil was more than strange. I asked him why no one else had discovered this and he just said, 'Perhaps no one is interested in looking."

"So, let me get this right," I questioned. "Forge is disclosing millions of dollars worth of precious metals but these records are for sales only?"

Emil nodded. "Yes, that's right. There are no records for mining. It all checks out, Eugene," he replied. "But, here's where it gets interesting though. Within the holdings of the company, Forge own shares in small-cap companies, 'Dragon Finance,' Griffin Pharma,' and 'Gladiator Fuel' and that's just the few I looked into, there's many more. I'd keep you up all night with the significance of all this but I haven't the patience nor the time, it took me a few days to work it all out, even then I thought I was going a little crazy myself. Eventually, I put all the company names into a simple crossword solver. I played around for some time until it came up with common denominators and 'FRG' came up every time. I continued adding in others and the same pattern was emerging in each case. And these are companies I've no knowledge about yet, but it got my attention."

I wondered if Emil was a little crazy at this point, but then again I thought you had to be a little mad being in the game we were, you had to look at things a little skewed. He'd come across the same damn thing I'd been looking at but had the tenacity to dig a little deeper than just posting a reminder note on a screen for himself.

You accepted getting things wrong nine times out of ten in this job but you only needed to get it right once and you had a breakthrough. That's how we worked in homicide, so I listened as Emil continued.

He was a convincing man and after he spoke we brought out the contents we'd taken from Spiel's office. I took a look at the bank statement. There were names, lots of them with money coming in and out, transactions Leon Spiel had made in the daily running of his practice. I handed it to Emil without thinking much to it and turned my attention to the index cards from the Rolodex, thumbing through names, not really knowing what I was looking for, but then Emil said, "Saltman,

now that's a name I've not heard for almost fifty years."
We both looked up at our employer.

"Vaschel Saltman. In Auschwitz, they just called him 'Vasch'. Back then he was just a young boy, maybe five or six years of age, and he was an unpopular child because of his father, 'Rudy Saltman," he said, the words with slowness and precision. "Rudy was a very unpleasant Kapo, another collaborator," he said, tilting the paper from side to side, as though his eyes were deceiving him. "Are you alright, Emil?" I asked.

"It's a terrible thing to have such memories, such terrors fill my dreams at night," he sat contemplating what he was holding within his hands. "You see this 'Kapo' was killed when Auschwitz was liberated in the January of 45, his killers didn't wear Nazi uniforms, they wore the striped clothing of the inmates, the same I wore myself, his own people killed him, the community he'd spent years oppressing. I know about Rudy Saltman. He's in The Sikora Files. Aleksy was very keen on that particular file. Saltman was a very dangerous man who protected his son with every means available to him. Vasch witnessed his father's murder, it must have been a dreadful thing for such a young boy to witness. You see, Saltman was beaten to death with the very same baton he'd wielded on his fellow captives," Emil said but, oddly, there was compassion in his voice. "Vasch must be in his fifties now. All this time… all this time."

It struck me Emil felt some guilt about Vaschel Saltman but I didn't push him on it, the man couldn't have done a thing about the situation even if he'd wanted to. I guess in such times, awful things happened and revenge on your oppressor was at the forefront of the thoughts of the hundreds, if not thousands, of unfortunate human beings who'd seen their loved ones marched off to the gas chambers by the likes of Rudy Saltman.

Emil broke the tension that had been building up in the room. "Right! We have a name and we need to find out why Vaschel Saltman's on Leon Spiel's bank account. I really need you to talk to that lawyer again. Can you arrange that, Eugene?"

The next morning, I rang Spiel's home number several times, no one answered. I rang his receptionist who informed me she'd not seen him and hadn't been able to contact him herself. It was frustrating but then later that day I took a call from Fin. "Gene, a body's been found in the water at the Manhattan Ferry Terminal. It's Spiel.

Looks like he was hit sometime in the night. There was a heavy fog in the early hours, so no one noticed him before," he said, disappointment in his voice. "Listen, I'll look after the Spiel job, get what I can and let's all collate what we have later. How about we meet at your place?"

***

Jody and I enjoyed sitting out on Sunday mornings in the grounds of Madison Square Park, we'd watch the world passing by and contemplate the past week. We'd pick up a couple of coffees at our favourite place *Grumpy's* and catch up. Although we lived together, our working lives meant we spent a lot of time apart and in Jody's case her shift patterns would change often. She worked in the Emergency Department in the New York Hospital in Queens, for over fifteen years now, it's how I met her. She'd been the acute care doctor on a stabbing victim I was tasked to interview. At the time my life *was* the job, I had nothing else going really, she kind of captivated me and I'd asked her out on a date the first time I met her. "I'm busy, I've patients to tend to," I recall her saying.

I'd thought that was just her way of rebutting my advances but she'd later found me in the hospital cafeteria and apologised for her apparent rudeness. I hadn't taken it that way but pushed for a date on the strength of it, she was a hell of a fine-looking lady, and the rest, as they say, is history.

We had our routines like every couple do, but living in the Flat Iron together was a little different to most, if you didn't know us and the jobs we did for a living, you could take our relationship as a little strange. It suited us anyway. I told her that Fin and Emil were coming round for dinner that night and we'd have a brainstorming session, get a handle on where we were at with the case. I said I'd get some Chinese food in, asking her preference.

As we walked through Madison Square Park it started raining a little and we both ran for cover, laughing as we went, like two teenagers. We weren't getting any younger but weren't of the age of giving up just yet. We'd both missed out on having children; the jobs had taken priority in our lives, so we just had each other to care for. Sunday mornings were our time but that wasn't to say a shift pattern or homicide hadn't broken into that either. We had a joint understanding though, one we called 'in the bag'. If something interrupted our routine we'd stow that one *in the bag,* to take another day. Importantly, we were happy within our relationship with one another, neither gave the other pressure, and we rarely had a bad word between us. I think that was because of mutual respect, anyway, we got on just fine.

Discarding the coffee cups in the nearest bin, I challenged her to a race, the last one back to reception would tidy the flat. I had an advantage though, I was wearing sneakers. Jody wore knee-length boots.

"You two crazy kids oughta take a brolly with you next time," Anthony, the concierge, commented as we passed through the foyer. It was an easy win for me, but in the end, we both readied the flat for our evening visitors.

***

Fin handed me a bottle of red wine whilst Emil brought flowers for Jody. I introduced them both.

"Thank you, Emil, I've heard a lot about you from Gene," she said, receiving the bouquet and smelling the blooms within.

Emil looked at me and questioned the shortening of my name. "You prefer Gene? Why didn't you tell me?" he smiled.

"It doesn't bother me what you call me, just don't call me too early in the morning," I responded. Jody pulled a face at me for my dumbass answer and took the flowers and their coats whilst I attempted to make amends by pouring them drinks.

We settled down at the table gathering the notes. Emil started by saying, "So, we know that Ilse Gerver was a guard at Belsen and admitted her war crimes on the videotape you both acquired. We have written testimony that should have been admitted from the original case from Wilhelm Becker that we could have used in a second hearing. Becker also identified Rudi Baumann as the SS guard in overall charge of Gerver. Your thoughts at this point, gentlemen, please," he said.

Fin answered first. "The fact she's dead doesn't help build our case but we can use what we have for the overall picture. What you've just said is solid, we can put that in the bank but nothing else is, as of yet, apart from Hans Schröder who you quite brilliantly tied to the hanging of the twenty-three Latvians."

I added, "Yeah, and we have him as the man who probably gave the 'Final Order' *and*, with no reason to disbelieve what they sent us over from the 'Wiesenthal Centre', also fleeing to Brazil via Paraguay."

Fin interjected: "A*nd,* we know the Belsen Commandant, Haas, signed off Schröder's papers which came from Nazi headquarters, the ones we believe Hitler himself ordered."

Not to be outdone, I responded, "We've also got the other connections; Otto Weiss and Schröder; there seemed to be a close relationship. I'm taking a look at Weiss who I believe was Schröder's bodyguard. It looks like he's running a business in Brazil with six other fellow Nazis."

Jody interrupted with a knock on the door. "Are you guys ready for Chinese food yet?" she asked.

"Please, come and sit down, we've taken over your home, let the three of us wait on you," Emil smilingly said whilst pouring a glass of wine for her.

The meal we had was wonderful, from a regular place of ours, and we ran over a few more things afterwards whilst Jody stacked the dishwasher with whatever plates we'd used. Fin had nothing positive about Spiel.

One to the head and he could have gone in the water almost anywhere around there, Homicide were checking the tides, then we spent the rest of the evening getting to know each other informally. Emil was impressed with Jody's job, Fin told a few rum stories that had happened many years back and we drank until Emil looked at the clock then worried about the time. "I must get home, Luiza will think I've another woman."

After he got home, Emil phoned back, telling me to thank Jody for her company and a lovely evening and then said, "Eugene, you're doing a fine job, I'm proud of the work we're all doing, now get yourself some sleep, we have much to do," and before he put the phone down I remembered to tell him, "There's one thing I didn't mention to you, Emil. I found a book in Otto Weiss's file case, titled, 'Albert Speer: Inside The Third Reich'. I've put it to one side, I thought it may be significant in some way."

"That's interesting Eugene, very interesting indeed, now get some sleep." He hung up and I smiled, I'd enjoyed the night's company, it wasn't often we entertained people, so it had been something different for the both of us.

Chapter 4

Animals and Men

Emil's computer had a virus, one that Luiza couldn't erase with the software that came with it, so I took it down to a local shop in Greenwich Harbor to try to resolve the problem. Whilst there, I asked if the technician could locate the actual website from which Emil had obtained the photograph of Josef Rösler.

"It shouldn't be a problem, we can just check the activity log, that'll show us the browsing history before we clean the machine, but it's a good job you asked me that before I started," he said. He went on to tell me it would take a few hours to run the scans and do the necessary work to get rid of the virus, so he'd just print off websites Emil may have visited over the past few weeks and I could then search them individually but warned me, I'd need a strong firewall and anti-virus when I did it. I didn't quite understand what he was saying and he knew that. Smiling he said, "It's ok, I'll set it all up and put McAfee on it for you,"

"Great," I replied, trying to appear like I knew what the hell he was talking about.

I took a walk into the village to kill a few hours, it was a beautiful place. I thought I'd bring Jody here one day for a meal. The blossoms had just fallen from the trees leaving a layer of pink and white over the neatly mown lawns, giving the place a feeling of enchantment. As I walked, I realised the value of my flat in New York would afford me something nice out here; maybe we might be having more than a meal sometime.

I phoned Emil to inform him about the computer and he told me he'd walk into town to join me. "I need to stretch my legs," he'd said, but by now I knew his intention, Macduff's was a little bolt hole of his. I think he'd spent most of his life attached by an umbilical cord to Luiza, in a nice kind of way that is, but I'd seen him make excuses to get out of the house for milk or some such thing, just to get a little time to himself.

Sure enough, after meeting he took me to Macduff's and told me, "I've come for a reason. Whilst I was researching Forge Ore, I did some digging into our list of German directors and found that not only was Josef Rösler a fervent Holocaust denier, the other directors were also. They were all members of HIAG, the Mutual Aid Association for the former SS. It was their veterans' organisation founded by former high ranking SS personnel, its idealism was to achieve both legal and economic historical rehabilitation for the Waffen-SS. Group membership was up to twenty thousand people, and it used its power and influence to lobby political parties and to deny the Holocaust had ever happened. They owned a publishing house and, just as before the war, their propaganda was printed and distributed across the world. The organisation was condemned in the West in its later years for its openly right-wing and extremist views." I sat silently listening to the information he offered. I couldn't believe what I was hearing.

"And Weiss?" I questioned, hoping he was one of them.

"Unfortunately not, I found nothing on him, he's still clean," he said.

I was curious. "But surely we can use this? We just need to find an angle to get in on." I didn't get any further, a call from the technician at the shop informed me that the computer and print-outs were ready for pick up so we both finished our drinks and headed back to the shop.

It looked like Emil had made some real progress by what he'd told me. This was a guy who'd employed me so he could put his feet up a little more in his old age, but I was guessing it may well have been his wife's idea to take on another investigator, not her tenacious husband.

We got the computer back and drove to Emil's place where I set it back up whilst sending him off to spend some time with Luiza. "You're retired, it's my job," I said whilst gently pushing him out of the study he affectionately called 'Harry.'

I sat down looking at the printouts and there were plenty of websites. I typed a few of them into the browser cautiously, I found sites that were clearly about Nazism, some historical and others simply fan sites. It was bizarre witnessing real people actually believing all this crap. With fingers crossed hoping the computer wouldn't crash, I clicked a few links within sites attempting to find the photograph of Josef Rösler. The guy in the computer store had told me I may see a warning appear which was generated by the anti-virus software and to just click the 'this time only' button, allowing it temporary access. It happened and I did what he said, then I began to read the pages. There was a lot of white supremacist hate speech and, in general, hatred seemed to be at the fore of it all. I hadn't worked in this line of work before but the 'cop within' thought that if it wasn't illegal to put this kind of crap out for anyone to see, it god damn well should be.

The organisation had spread across the world, it was by no means in its infancy, it was huge, it actively promoted racism, anti-Semitism and ultra-nationalism. In fact, I noticed there was actually a group called 'The Ultras' and couldn't help but shake my head in disbelief. I dragged my mind back to the task in hand, remembering what Emil had said about HIAG and got down to work. Most of the sites had a search engine within them so you could look inside the website for particular words, phrases, or names. I typed in Josef Rösler on 'The Ultras' site and his photograph popped up, the same one Emil had found. I roamed around the site reading things here and there until a link directed me to a speech made by Rösler. It was in German so I couldn't understand it but I made a copy of the web page on a floppy disk with the idea of finding a translator later on.

Emil re-entered the room, "How are you getting on?" He just couldn't keep away, his instinct telling him to be involved, to do something, and I for one wasn't about to stop the guy.

Kaspar Stahnke was a moderator on 'The Ultras' website. I asked Emil, who'd sat to the side of me, "Do you think we should make some sort of contact with him?" He sat considering my idea, seemingly knowing my intentions. "Let's look into him first, Eugene, get some information of who he is and what he's about. Every contact we make must have solid foundations."

Of course, I agreed, it was something I'd thought of doing anyway, but I wanted to broach the idea with him first, after all this was his work, I couldn't just dive in making decisions without running them by him first. I thought Fin could be of use with it also, his way of approaching contacts was an asset to any investigation, he was good at it, an actor of the highest order.

I called him to let him know. "Fin, I'm gonna need your help, I want to get close to a guy, his name's 'Kaspar Stahnke,' he's a moderator on a Neo Nazi website. I'm going to do a little digging into him first though and I'll find out as much as I can but I think we need to gain his confidence and if necessary, befriend him," I said.

"That's fine by me, Gene, just tell me when and where, I'll be there."

A simple search of Stahnke's name returned another webpage called 'Six Degrees' I dug a little into this site, it was based on the six degrees of separation concept, listing friends and family members, importantly it allowed external contacts to join the site, it worked like a college bulletin board, people posted notes and memos to one another. I filled in my application with a false identity and awaited confirmation of membership approval. Emil came in with a tea, I let him know my plans. I tried explaining the theory behind the Six Degrees concept but he was an old man, his idea of interaction was a letter or telephone call and even that was a stretch, but in fairness, this was a little new to me too, so I wasn't exactly the best tutor. I was tired and it was getting late so I said my farewells and headed back to Greenwich station to catch the train home. I called Jody and let her know not to cook, "I'll get a pickup from 'Marty's," I told her, "run a bath, relax and I'll see you in an hour."

I fell asleep on the train and missed my stop, getting off at 28th Street, deciding to walk the mile home to wake me up a little, it was a fresh night. Luckily, I'd brought a jacket and pushed my hands deep into the pockets to keep them warm.

Whilst I was working on the Kaspar Stahnke lead, Fin concentrated all his efforts on Vaschel Saltman, ploughing through the Rolodex of phone numbers and files we'd taken from Leon Spiel's office. He'd found a discarded post-it note which gave him his first lucky break, the note had a telephone number on, it was the local Synagogue and, after a few enquiring calls, an address presented itself. The cantor had volunteered Saltman's information with enthusiasm, believing the call was about a job offer. That white lie got our foot in the door; we just had to work out how to approach him now. We couldn't go in all guns blazing and heavy-handed, we'd have to work a way of extracting as much information out of Saltman as we possibly could. We eventually decided it would call for deceit being played but we needed to talk to Emil, he'd know how to get under the skin of our connection to the deceased lawyer.

We spoke in-depth together, all three with differing views that all came together as one in the end. I still had my NYPD badge and Fin had a soundproof office at his home. His son had once used it as a recording studio and it would only take a few hours to make it look and feel like a Police interrogation room. The consensus was to bluff it out and set about our work. Fin also had a hood he'd acquired as a Bronx cop, he told me he'd used it on several occasions. I wondered what the hell my colleague was capable of but I had to trust him, Emil had and that was good enough reason. An ex-US Navy SEAL, he was clearly capable of handling himself, it was how far he'd go with Saltman that worried me a little. Deep down I knew we'd have to go to that place at some point but it still felt a little uncomfortable. Being so relatively new out of the job, I still retained that cops' ethos. I guess I'd never been a fan of private detectives until I became one myself.

Fin and I planned the 'hit'. We'd take him by force to Fin's house handcuffed, drugged and hooded. We both knew what we were doing wasn't conventional, but it was our only option to get complete control over

Saltman, and our only way of connecting the solicitor Spiel to Otto Weiss, if a connection existed.

The night we decided to run the hit was dreary and raining, we'd planned our method of capture, both Fin and I wore balaclava's, we looked like we were about to storm the 'Iranian Embassy' and the rain came down in torrents. Both of us thought of calling the whole thing off for another night but then he turned the corner, as we'd been informed he would, coming back from his nightly visit to the synagogue. The cantor had supplied us with a lot of useful information, we thought without realising he was doing it, but now it looked like he'd presented him on a plate to us. We looked at each other, nodding in agreement to go for it then got out of the car. As Saltman, listening to his 'Walkman', crossed the road toward us, Fin coolly walked by him then abruptly turned around. In a world of his own, it was easy for me to block his path, stopping him dead in his tracks and Fin came up from behind ready to administer the chloroform. The sudden realisation of the situation dawned upon Saltman's face and he attempted to push me away but I was ready for him and a quick side step left him unbalanced. Fin was strong, as soon as he got a grip on him, the soaked rag did its work.

"Get his legs, he's out cold, let's not draw attention to ourselves here," Fin said as we dragged and shoved the limp body into the rear of the car.

"He's a hell of a weight," I muttered.

Fin grunted, "That's why I gave him a good soaking of chloroform, I don't want him waking, he looks like he could give us a little trouble."

Whilst I drove, Fin administered a little more chloroform to make sure Saltman didn't surprise us by waking up. He worked fast, binding his arms and legs, placing a mask ready to pull down over his face if he woke, we didn't want to suffocate the guy and importantly didn't want him getting a visual on us. As I pulled up the drive to the house, Saltman stirred a little, so Fin administered a little more chloroform.

"That should do it, we'll get him in and settle down, then bring him round," Fin instructed. Lifting him between us to the room, somehow he seemed even heavier than before. "He'd have given us a hell of a fight, the guy's a man mountain. The cantor said he was carrying a bit of extra weight but he must be three hundred pounds or more," I said as Fin ensured our captive was bound tightly in the interrogation chair. We both knew what we were about to do wasn't by the book, the boundaries we'd be crossing were ones we couldn't easily come back from. We'd discussed this before the hit and both agreed that a greater good would come of it. Placing our masks on, I wafted the smelling salts beneath his nose and he stirred a little, but not as I thought he would. I attempted to give him a little more and that's when he headbutted me square on the nose. I felt the bone crack as his forehead slammed into the bridge of my nose then he violently shook the chair attempting to free himself, but Fin had tied him in good. I held my nose as the blood flowed. The energy this guy had was incredible. Dragging the hood over Saltman's eyes as he struggled, Fin pulled his gun from its holster and jammed it against our incredible hulk's head.

"You've got five seconds to calm the fuck down or I'm gonna put a hole in your head we can take a look through," he said, clicking the hammer back on the revolver. The chair became still. "Who the hell are you?" our detainee uttered.

"You've broken my nose you son of a bitch," I said in some discomfort then slapped him around the head.

"What do you want from me?" he said as Fin increased the pressure of the gun barrel to his temple.

"You shot a fuckin' dog! You're going to tell me exactly who employs you, and don't think for one minute I won't empty your brains all over this floor," he said.

"I don't know what you're talking about, I didn't shoot any god damn dog," he replied.

I opened the syringe case. I'd heard of sodium thiopental before, it was an old method of weakening the resolve of a subject making them more compliant to pressure. The theory was that lying being more complex than not lying, people under its influence were more likely to tell the truth. Fin had acquired it from a contact he'd made in New York.

Saltman began to struggle in the chair, making it difficult for Fin to stick him with the needle. The butt of Fin's gun across the bridge of his nose stopped that, instantly.

"You can call that a warning. If you struggle, I'm going to hurt you, and I'm going to hurt you badly," Fin threatened. By now my nose was aching badly and I was finding it difficult to concentrate. Fin glared at me for some encouragement so I took my gun out and waved it around. I knew then it was the turning point, there was no going back.

Leaning in close to Saltman, I said, "You have allegiances to these scum bags, first of all, I want you to tell me why then I want you to tell me who?"

"I'm telling you nothing, you don't know who you're messing with, you're dead men walking," he announced as Fin stuck the needle into his arm. I slapped his face. "Fuck you," he replied. He was gutsy; I had to give him that.

We waited whilst the drug started to kick in a little and, as planned, we were going to put the fear of God into him.

Fin explained. "I'm gonna tell you what we're going to do to you now Vaschel. People like you mastered this little torture technique, they called it 'the post'," he said whilst lifting the hood from his face so he could see clearly what was in front of him.

"See that hook up there on the wall?" Fin hissed. "I'm going to hang you up there and watch your shoulders rip from out of their sockets, you son of a bitch," His tone made me shudder a little, I could sense the hatred within, it made me think he was really going to do it. I stepped forward, "Vasch, nobody knows you're here, nobody fucking cares, and we can do what the hell we want to. Believe me, my colleague here, he's a very capable man, this is his bag, his thing. You know, I actually believe he enjoys it." I laughed a little as I told him, "You'll be screaming for your god damn life in just a few moments, or you could be a smart guy and tell us exactly what we want to know."

"Please, let me out of here," he whimpered, his head now bent down as he began talking. "They murdered my father, they tortured him in front of me and then they hung him."

It was an attempt to gain sympathy and Fin wasn't impressed. "We know all that and we don't care, who are you fucking working for?" he said pointing the butt of the gun at Saltman's nose, readying himself to administer another blow.

"No, please! I work for the Mosque. I work the computers for them," he said.

"How do you know Josef Rösler?" Fin demanded.

"I don't, I swear."

"Hook this guy up, he's fucking lying to us," Fin threatened and we both began lifting him towards the hook as he screamed out loud. I was nervous; I didn't know how far Fin would go. I'd seen photographs of this method of torture before, it was, without doubt, terrifying, your arms would rip out of their sockets with the weight of your own body working against you. I hoped he was going to do the right thing; I didn't want this on my conscience.

"Alright, I'll tell you, please!" he said, the fear of what was about to happen to him almost choking him.

As we sat him back down, Fin demanded, "Did you phone Leon Spiel?"

"Yes," he nodded.

"You got him to get the address of Mr Janowitz and told him your name was Wise, is that right?" he asked with menace. Saltman looked at me, looking for some assistance.

"Don't look at me!" I shouted. "Answer the god damn question! Did you tell Leon Spiel you were Mr Wise?"

He capitulated. "Yes."

Fin pressed home our advantage, his nose almost touching Saltman's. "You're going to tell us everything you know, every fucking last thing or I swear to god I'm going to hang you on that hook and watch the life drain from you."

There was silence for a while and I spent it thinking I'd known the hit would be bad but hadn't been sure how far Fin would go though. My suspicions of the Ernst Schaefer case revisited me and it was clear that Fin was capable of killing Saltman, as I guessed he had with Schaefer. He had that intensity about him that couldn't be restrained and I sensed something else, a kind of animal instinct emanating from him when pushed. It shocked me if I'm honest, but I knew these methods were the only way of extracting exactly what we wanted. The thought did cross my mind as I looked up at the hook, 'are we any better than those bastards?' and I worried that there didn't seem to be a line to stop us from crossing over. I quickly put it to one side as Fin filled the void and asked, "You know they've found Leon Spiel's body floating in the Hudson, are you aware of that?"

I felt the need to say something but could only throw in, "We're gonna find your DNA all over that body, one way or the other you're going down, Vaschel."

Tears rolled down Saltman's cheeks. "I swear I didn't shoot the dog."

"But you were there," Fin kept the pressure on.

"Yes."

"Who shot the fuckin' dog?" he demanded.

"It was Baumann. He did it to warn you off. He meant to kill him as a warning and would have if Lars hadn't intervened and ruined his aim. You should take notice, you're not dealing with two-bit criminals, they'll kill you and they'll kill your fucking family, you've no idea what you're messing with, this is bigger than you can ever imagine. I'm a dead man talking to you, you're dead men, we're all fucking dead men," he said, bowing his head, sobbing.

I tried to push him further. "You said Baumann. Is that Rudi Baumann? Vaschel! Is that Rudi Baumann?"

"I don't know. Everyone just calls him Baumann."

"And who's 'Lars'?" I continued.

"I don't know, he just said his name was Lars."

"Who killed Spiel?"

"I don't know, I really don't know, I wasn't there."

Fin interceded. "I'm going to ask you another question and I want you to think very carefully before you answer because I swear to God I'll hang you on that fucking hook. Who is Wise? Tell me," a pause was left, Saltman looked afraid. I wasn't sure if the fear was for the hook or the ramification of the information he was about to offer up.

"Otto Weiss was an SS Officer at Belsen, my father knew him. I was only six years of age when they liberated the camp and my childhood was destroyed in that single moment when they killed my father. I left with hatred in my soul because of what they did to my father and I always wanted revenge. I signed up with 'The Ultras'. It was just a job, they needed an IT specialist. At first, I helped them set up the website and got to know Josef Rösler through that, but then I was put in contact with the company," he said.

"WHAT COMPANY!?" Fin bawled at him.

"FORGE ORE!" he shouted back, with a combination of anger and fear. He took a breath and continued. "They wanted to modernise, get up to date with technology, everyone else was doing it at the time, websites, things like that. Weiss knew who I was, called me his 'Good Little Jew'. He knew my father. When I started working for the company, he made enquiries about my name. My tattoo confirmed my identity to him and he linked me to my father. Once he knew exactly who I was, he asked me if I was a national socialist. He was laughing. I told him they murdered my father and that I hated Jews as much as he did. He asked if I was like my father, a good little Kapo. I told him I wanted to be." Vaschel began to sob.

"You know we can't let you go, don't you," Fin said abruptly, "But I've told you everything you asked me, please, they'll kill me anyway," he pleaded as I looked at Fin, fearing what was about to possibly happen. The plan was to keep him dosed, the sodium thiopental would erase the memory of what had happened, but Fin kept the pretence of violence and the threat to kill up, we'd agreed stress was the key factor in the interrogation of him.

"We're looking for the man who ultimately gave the order to kill all of the remaining Jews in Europe, in all the concentration camps, that order was given by an SS man," Fin informed him.

"They dehumanised my father," was all he said.

Fin looked at me and walked away, I followed out the door, "What are we going to do with him," I asked.

"We'll let him sleep for a while then dump him back home, he won't remember a thing," he quietly replied.

"I'd hate to get on the wrong side of you, Fin," I said, contemplating our situation.

"This is the job, Gene, it's what we're signed up for, these people aren't your nice everyday criminals, they'd stab you in the back as soon as look at you. Get into another mindset with this," he offered.

"Yes, I know," I replied. He was right.

Later that night, he made a meal for Vasch, putting an effort into it, feeding him by hand as a father would his son. It was then I realised Fin took no pleasure from his work; he was just professional at what he did. That same night, we dosed him up again and dropped an unconscious Vaschel Saltman, back outside his flat, he'd wake the next morning wondering what the hell had happened to him, at worst, he'd recall the men in hoods, but he'd remember nothing of the interrogation that had taken place. I thought it had gone well

"It's a good job we got the sodium thiopental," Fin said knowingly, and as I looked at my partner a thought crossed my mind, 'he'd have done it as well.'

Chapter 5

The New Radicals

Kaspar Stahnke was a mid-thirties, long-haired, scruffy-looking bully, one you could instantly tell would shy away from a fight if the numbers didn't work in his favour. I'd planted a seed on the 'Six Degrees' website after receiving my acceptance email, it wasn't rocket science working out how to get into the head of these kind of people, you just had to say the right thing at the right time to the right person. I'd added a comment to one of his posts, and several other members had joined in the thread. Kasper followed what I said with great enthusiasm and, from that point onwards, my interests lay only with him. I'd logged in under an alias, 'Bruno Lange,' I thought it sounded relatively German and therefore safe. It appeared most on Six Degrees were posting under aliases or names that seemed dubious; their so-called alter egos. Stahnke used his real name though, arrogance on his behalf but a godsend to me, it would have been a difficult puzzle if he'd given another. I passed comment on a number of his posts on the board, and after a few weeks, he began shooting the breeze about himself, informing me all about 'The New Radicals,' as he called the followers of the Ultras and Six Degrees web forums he was the moderator for. He shared his beliefs of radicalising the world, views I found quite disturbing, but I followed and encouraged, remembering all the time Emil's words, not to burn any bridges. Over just a few weeks I gained his confidence as was my intent, building trust between the two of us, using the skills I'd learned over the many years to ensnare people. He believed I was a mid-twenties young German, looking for direction in life. I'd learnt through the internet that this kind of relationship, between neo Nazis, rarely led to a meeting, it was all done at an arm's length, the tutor could then just disappear at any given moment into the ether of the internet, never to be seen or heard of again. Like Fin, I'd become quite the actor though, basing myself on the character Hando in the film Romper Stomper which I'd sat and watched on videotape one evening to get a feel for the character and what I was about to get into. Jody wasn't best pleased, but after I told her my purpose she agreed to have an early night and leave me to it.

I gave Stahnke the belief that I liked hurting people. I'd told him I enjoyed the feeling of power it gave me and, slowly, an alliance was formed between two strangers across the internet but only one knew who the other really was.

I filled Emil in on my daily conversations with Stahnke, reassuring him I wasn't leading him too far too soon, but although I wasn't quite clear of my intention at that point, I was driving down a familiar road. I received a notification post on 'Six Degrees' written by Stahnke one Sunday morning, just one of his normal white supremacy posts directed at the board and not particularly to myself, but I knew he'd be putting things in because of me, wanting to impress his new recruit to 'The New Radicals.'

As I was reading it, he mentioned something that caught me by surprise, "The ultimate betrayal is of your own kind, and nobody betrayed their own more so than the Architect". He'd quoted it within context to some other irrelevant post. My mind raced to find an adequate response. Who was this 'Architect', had I missed something? I realised my best reply was to say nothing at all, but I thought back to that book I found in Otto

Weiss's casefile, the one I'd been meaning to read for several months, but hadn't. Was he talking of Speer, he was the only Architect I could think of? Why would he be suggesting Albert Speer betrayed his own kind in such a way? I understood Speer had turned on his fellow Nazi's at the Nuremberg Trials but had always assumed he was a hero to these kind of people.

It puzzled me somewhat, so I decided there and then to pick that book up and read it to unearth more about Speer, maybe after all there was a reason Aleksy Markowski had placed the book within the file. I took a phone call from Emil and decided to visit him that afternoon, it was a sunny day and I thought I'd give him an excuse to get out of the house for an hour or so, it sounded like he needed it. I caught the train to Greenwich and called into Idar Court. Greeted by Luiza with her customary friendly face, Max wasn't his usual excitable self though, not surprisingly, and he looked a little sorry for himself, so I made a big fuss of him to cheer him up a little, the poor guy had been in the wars. Emil grabbed a jacket and shouted through to the kitchen, "Luiza, Eugene and I are just taking a walk, we need to discuss the case and my legs need some exercise."

"Yes, Emil, don't drink too much! You must think I don't understand your little secrets but go, enjoy yourselves, your dinner will be ready when you come home," she replied. Emil whispered to me like a schoolboy, "Come on, let's go before she changes her mind."

As we walked, I told him of the comment Stahnke had made about 'The Architect' in the forum. He listened with curiosity and, as I finished, he said, "Let me tell you a little story, I was once told by Aleksy that 'The Odessa' were real people. Frederick Forsyth hadn't been that far from the truth when he wrote his book. I've read about Albert Speer, he was a very curious man, I'd encourage you to read the book and when you've finished pass it onto me, I'd like to read it myself."

"I've two copies, Emil, I bought a duplicate from the book store in Greenwich, the one in the file was a little dog eared. I'll bring it round," I replied.

We had some beers and talked about the case, and also of Speer, then I walked him back home where Luiza was waiting on the doorstep. "Oh Eugene, never get married," he said, clasping an arm around my shoulder. "I love the woman but she frightens me sometimes," he said with a grin on his face. I said my farewell and as he walked towards the house I could hear him muttering, "Yes, Luiza, Emil's had two beers," which was a white lie, we'd had three.

"Go on in, your dinner is on the table waiting for you, you can walk Max after you've had it," she said, whilst smiling and waving to me. You could see they took good care of each other; they were soul mates, and I knew Luiza worried a great deal for Emil, especially after he was jumped by a gang of young Nazis in Venezuela and received a beating so bad he'd spent some time in an intensive care unit. I thought about that as I sat on the train back home. He'd been through so much in his life and the lowest specimens of humanity had beaten this increasingly frail old man within an inch of his life, it made me more determined to fulfil our goal.

Later that night, in bed, I started reading the Speer autobiography, written in Spandau Prison during his twenty-year incarceration after the Nuremberg Trials. I read the 'Foreword', normally I'd skip past that part to the first chapter, but I didn't want to miss a thing that may have some consequence. First published in 1969, a year later it was translated into English. I was hoping it would take me inside the inner circle of the 3rd Reich. I glanced over the cover, it looked compelling, then the phone rang in the hall. Jody was just coming to bed, "Who will it be at this time of night?" she asked, a concerned look on her face. She was often on call, and even when she wasn't there was always a chance they'd call her anyway so there was a little hesitancy when a call came in so late. I picked up. "It's Emil, I'm sorry to ring so late." I let Jody know so she could relax.

"Eugene, you said you were going to read the Speer book," he began.

"Yes, I was just reading the first chapter," I interrupted.

"That's good, but I want you to know a few things before you read on, things I know about Albert Speer, things that he may or may not admit to within *his* book."

I sat down on the side chair we'd recently bought for the hall; I had a feeling this call may take some time.

"Albert Speer was in Auschwitz on several occasions. I once saw him whilst I was put on work duty in Kanada, he was watching what was going on all around him. Later, in the Nuremberg trials, he would give testimony that he didn't know what was going on but that he should have. This was his lie, a total and utter lie, Eugene. Albert Speer knew everything that was going on at Auschwitz, he gave the orders to conscript more personnel from all over Europe, this of course was against their will and they were used for labour work at places like Monowitz Concentration Camp. I told you I haven't read the book you hold, which is true, but I have read of the man, and of the lies he told whilst placating the judges at his trial. He gave them what they wanted to hear. My gut instinct tells me it had to be a high ranking officer within the SS or the regime that would have given that final order. I want you to proceed with this case believing it was Speer who gave the order, perhaps one approach would be to try and disprove it was him," he said, which surprised me a little as Emil was a man that didn't work off chances, possibilities or maybe's, he always struck me as an evidence-based detective. "Ok, Emil, can I ask you why, why we would assume it was Speer?" I asked.

"Eugene, the fact he was an architect may be coincidental but he was also the Reich Minister of Armaments and they don't come much higher. There was something about the man that has always intrigued me, he was the anomaly within the Nuremberg trials, and all these years I've always believed he pulled the wool over their eyes. It's something that has gnawed away at me. I think he has something to do with all of this. It's played on my mind today, when you told me about your conversation with Kaspar Stahnke, it set in motion thoughts and memories, ones I really don't want to recall, but he was a Nazi, possibly the most intelligent of them all,

and his ambition was ceaseless. This is our opportunity to cancel the 'Speer myth'. I know the man is dead, but in my mind, he got away with his role in the Holocaust, and although we can't prosecute and get some meaningful justice, we can use what we find and move forward with it," he said, weariness weighting his words.

"You sound tired, Emil, get some sleep, it's late. I'll come round in the morning and we can discuss this further, now get it out of your mind and go to bed," I told him.

"Yes, Eugene, you're like Luiza, always right, goodnight young man," with that the line went dead and I went back to my reading.

The next morning, I woke early and made a pot of coffee and sat looking out over Broadway and the crowds below. I continued to read, making notes as I turned each page; Speer had a friend who was a sculptor, he had a pilot's licence, his subordinate Fritz Sauckel was sentenced to death at the trials and on the 16th October was hanged, ten others were hanged at the same time. I thought I needed to notate every little detail and started from the very beginning but the book wasn't necessarily in any sort of date order, it would flit between the war years then return to his youth. He was bullied by his brothers as a young boy which obviously affected his character and he, like Hitler, was a loner. He stood alone in his guilt of the war crimes and deliberately set himself against the others on trial, yet Emil's words reflected Speer's words and I realised

Emil had wanted me to have some kind of insight into the man before I read Speer's testimony of events. It was Hitler and Speer who ordered foreign workers into Germany by forced labour and reading the book, Speer gave a defence he was only carrying out Hitler's demands.

I sat wondering about going down blind alleys, and being warned not to by Emil himself, and yet it seemed that's exactly what I was doing, on his own say so. At the time I just couldn't see where it was all leading, but I endured, I'd get there in the end, I always did.

My Sundays had turned into somewhat of a ritual, meeting Emil with Jody, sometimes on my own, other times he'd come over to the Flat Iron and have a meal, but we always took an hour to walk down to a bar and have our talk. Our friendship developed pretty quickly, and I realised he'd never shared his experiences of the war before, and in me, he found someone he could relate to, he'd carried his burden through life. We'd always start our conversations talking about the Sikora Files, and follow up with some small talk of baseball, but I knew he needed to talk, and I was there for him as a friend, listening. He knew he could trust me.

He called me Filip by mistake one day as we sat around the dinner table. I looked up and caught Luiza's eye, she dismissively shook her head but he'd told me of his brother and how close he'd been to him, it gave me some comfort knowing that he was so relaxed within my company and that he could once again, at least for a short period, feel his beloved brother's company. He didn't even notice his mistake, several minutes later he'd refer to me by my own name once more, his lapse in memory only a temporary thing. Somewhere in his thought patterns, the conversation made him think of his brother, and he'd been lost in the moment, smiling. He told me he and Luiza had paid a visit to Auschwitz shortly after he'd received the first letter from Aleksy Markowski, he'd wanted to re-acquaint himself with his memories, and wrongly believed it would help. "It was a disaster, Luiza hated the place, I went with an intention, but came away with nothing. I was walking through the rooms and came across the shoe room, where they stored the thousands of pairs of shoes stolen from the victims, by chance we saw a pair of red shoes which stood out from the others, it reminded me of a family I'd once known. I'll never forget their names,

Rohaan and Meela Emery. I met them as they first reached the ramp in Auschwitz, they were so confused and scared, I tried to help them, somehow they managed to get through the selection process and, for a while, they settled into a daily routine within the camp. Meela reminded me of my little sister Anna, she was a real joy, always playing as children should, but like my sister the Nazis exterminated them. Little Meela's red shoes stared back at me through the glass when we revisited Auschwitz Birkenau that day and I found it hard to control my emotions, she was just a child. What harm could a child do?" he said, his voice ladened with an awful sadness.

Our talks became an important part of our friendship, and one night Emil was quite distressed as I listened to his recollections of Speer at Auschwitz, all those years ago. Talk of Hitler's architect had triggered nightmares that Luiza was now well aware of. He spoke for some time, describing in great detail exactly what he'd been through. "I've never spoken to anyone other than Lars about what I witnessed, Eugene, and that was many years ago, I thought I'd left it all behind, but the nightmares are becoming more regular. You see, Speer witnessed things, he knew of the terrible things they were doing to us. I'd been tasked to work in Kanada, sorting the many items stolen from the new arrivals, as I told you, but what I didn't tell you is the thing that's affecting my dreams," he said then paused to gather himself.

Knowing he was going through much more than I could ever comprehend, I took the opportunity to tell him, "Emil, I consider you a friend, if it helps you can tell me anything you need. I know you can't talk to Luiza about these things, if there's anything you need to get out, please use me as a sounding board." He nodded acceptance and said, "I was taken to Auschwitz 3, the Monowitz labour camp one day, Speer was inspecting the place, ascertaining if more labour was needed or if the workforce was performing to the standard the Führer expected. There was an old man who'd been working on the castings, his age was affecting his work rate and I saw Speer pointing to him, he'd noticed I'm sure. Later after Speer had left, the old man was taken outside by an SS guard. I recall the words the guard spoke, they haunt my dreams. He said, 'Come along, father, this is all too much for you, let us find you an easier job,' and he casually walked him out of the building with a caring arm around his shoulder to gain his trust. He shot him in the courtyard. To talk to the old man in such a way, friendly, like he was doing him a favour by taking him away from the hard labour and then cynically put a Luger to the back of his head and extinguish his life was just one of the cruellest things I bore witness to. The others, heads down, focussed hard on their work, to make eye contact in these circumstances could be a death sentence, you understand. As I was close at hand, I was ordered to get rid of the body. I relive this scene most nights at the moment, waking not as you'd think when the shot rang out, but at the sound of the old man's limp body crashing onto the cobbles. The following day, I was given duties in the wash house, sorting through prisoner uniforms, washing them so they could be re used on new entrants. I came across a stained jacket, still wet with blood on the back of it. I thought about the old man, not twelve hours earlier wearing it. His body now lay in a pile awaiting the incinerator. You see, the uniform had been worth more to the Nazis than the man himself, it had a value, they saw nothing of use within the man who'd worn it. They'd taken everything they could from him, his possessions, his labour and now they would take his hair and his teeth. When he became a burden to them they cynically exterminated his life, his worth to them was one single bullet, and even that became too much of an expense for the Nazi's so Rudolf Höss developed other methods of killing people, ways that were easier for the perpetrators, not the victims."

I tried imagining what Emil had gone through, but I just couldn't put myself in his shoes, so awful were the crimes, even trying to think about it was difficult. I guess, like everybody else of my generation, I'd put those war crimes into the black and white world of yesteryear, a time before, that somehow gave us an excuse to think of them differently to the crimes of today. It was history, but not that far in the distant past that you didn't feel some perspective to it all. I was born in 1943. The Holocaust occurred within my lifetime, taking place when I was a child, so whether I wanted to be or not I was connected. But, from my talks with Emil, I knew I wanted to be, it was important. I felt our lives were entwined somehow. Whilst I was being brought up in safety and love, Emil and all the others were enduring a hell that was recent enough to still influence the world, as we were now discovering.

Jody would ask me what Emil and I spoke of, but I chose to keep that part of his life between him and me alone, he hadn't opened up so I could go telling people. He'd said he wanted me to remember what he told me because "What happened shouldn't be forgotten." I realised I had a responsibility, his life wasn't to be forgotten, it was to be remembered and documented, he'd chosen me because we were alike, he knew I'd recall everything and ensure every emotion, feeling and meaning would go into my notes, an unofficial biography for a friend. I knew what Emil had inherited and how important the work was to history. "The evil still exists, it must be hunted down," he'd once said, and I knew it was important to follow through with our work, not just for Emil and Aleksy, but for the millions who didn't get the opportunity to see justice.

Jody wasn't pleased with my new look. I had a broken nose and I'd told her of my intention to get my hair cut down to the bone.

I wanted to look a little like Russell Crow's character Hando in Romper Stomper. I'd told her it was only short term and that I'd grow it back, which appeased her a little, but I could still see her looking at me with unforgiving eyes. My plan was simple; to infiltrate Stahnke's network of friends and, importantly, to find out what Josef Rösler's role was within the New Radicals. I knew it was a reach, but I had to give it a try. If we were to get to Otto Weiss, who we believed to be the bodyguard of Hans Schröder, then we'd have to take a few risks, and things just wouldn't present themselves on a plate for us, we'd have to work hard at connecting the pieces of the puzzle. Some wouldn't fit, sure, but I was certain what we had so far was correct and, besides, the Wiesenthal Centre wouldn't have given us misinformation.

Fin had been working separately, he spent his weekends with his children which was understandable, but he came to Idar Court to inform us of some new information he'd been working on, information that fell smack bang into what Emil and I had been researching.

"I've been looking into an operation they called Project Safe Haven, first discovered by a French intelligence officer working for their Deuxieme Bureau. It seems an Obergruppenführer Schneid and other Nazi's had a plot to smuggle gold, patents and art out of Germany through Switzerland which at the time was the world's banker and it held millions of dollars of gold in its vaults. , The aim was to re-establish the Nazi party as an underground movement," Fin explained.

Emil interrupted, "Yes, this is what I was telling Eugene, the Odessa, it was all real. Now Findlay, will you be telling me next that the SS and the collaborating industrialists made a plan to distribute the spoils of war?"

Fin smiled. "Exactly, Emil, this was the plan, and we're working the right pages with Forge Ore," he said. "I believe they were founded from Nazi plunder, and I'm currently working on linking Hans Schröder to Project Safe Haven, which I may add I don't think will take very long," he said with the confidence of a man who already knew but just needed confirmation.

Later that night, after Fin had left and Luiza was busying herself in the kitchen, Emil pulled me to one side, "I may be an old man, Eugene, but inside, I still feel like the young boy I was. Yes, my bones ache a little, but I still think and breathe the same way as I did back then. I see my brother in the man walking down the street, every now and then, just as he was all those years ago and it makes me stop to see if it's really him. I find myself deliberately looking at every little girl with curly blonde hair, to see if I can catch a single glimpse of my little Anna. Only last week, I saw a man younger than myself, by quite some years, but he wore the same spectacles and had the looks of my father, but you see mankind is made in such a way that when you lose your most dear family, the reminders are all around you, to me they are blessings. But not to all people. I know my friend Lars was haunted by such things, glimpses of the past, reminders of who you were and who you still are. But imagine looking at a boy of 19 years of age today, identical to your brother who died fifty years ago, it's one of life's miracles, and we all have them," he said, and he was right, I'd seen people who were not just like my parents in looks, they even dressed like them, they'd have the same eyes, nose, cheekbones and the same features, but as far as I knew, they bore no relation to me. They say each one of us has a doppelgänger on this planet.

Emil told me, "Life has a way of healing you, no matter how badly you've been damaged. I know from my own experience of how I healed myself, although not completely, I don't think I'll ever be completely healed, but because I did the right things at the right time, it gave me the opportunity to have a good life with Luiza. You learn over time to endure, to be able to continue and tolerate. In life, you must do that."

That week, I was tasked to drive Emil and Luiza to the airport to meet his old friend Lars Kowalski, it was a pretty memorable ride, I'd not seen Emil so apprehensive and nervous before, he was excited at the same time, like a young boy. He was so anxious to get to the airport, he was giving instructions on the quickest route and talking excitedly like I'd never been to JFK before, but I let him enjoy the moment, after all this was someone important to him, really important.

As Lars walked through the arrival gates with his bags, looking from side to side for us, Emil ran over to him throwing his arms around his old friend, sobbing openly, both men sat down in the middle of the floor, unable to stand as the emotion took hold of them. Luiza pulled my arm as I went to help. "Let them have the moment," she said and I took a step back. I watched Emil touching Lars face as a brother would after a long absence. "You look good, just as I remember you," he told him.

"I feel old, and you, you look so healthy, you've put some weight on since I last saw you," Lars commented as they both smiled at each other. I thought about how he must have looked after Auschwitz and realised it was a compliment. What these two men had endured was unthinkable, I got a little choked up myself seeing Emil in such a way and Luiza noticed, grabbing hold of my hand. She gave Lars a welcoming hug and I grabbed the suitcases, walking them to the car, Emil followed arm in arm with Luiza and Lars.

I'd listened closely to all that Emil had told me, all the things he'd not been able to share with his own wife and children, I felt great pride that he'd chosen me to share it with, and although upsetting to hear, in a way it brought me a new understanding of not only the Holocaust but of war in general. All wars are simply an excuse to kill people, in one form or another; it was Emil that made me think that way. I guess being on homicide, I'd gotten used to death and seeing it in all its various guises, yet the way Emil explained and walked you through the experiences of his life was different. Like a good book, you could feel, smell and taste it, your senses became alive learning of all the evil things that happened and, because of my closeness, I began to feel a real hatred towards those people that perpetrated the crimes as I'd never done before on homicide. The job was one thing, I could leave it behind at the office when I went home, but I had to be careful with this case, as I realised it'd become personal. I knew Jody wouldn't like that, so I thought about what I'd say in our conversations before we had them.

My mind was becoming overwhelmed by the case, and I had to try to at least try to have a normal life at home. I didn't even tell Emil how I felt, he'd have blamed himself thinking our conversations had manifested in my hatred. I wasn't a stupid man though, I was a thinking cop, I knew what it was, and I knew how to play it, I could utilise it in the next stage of our investigation, my only worry was could I snap back out of it afterwards. I'd think about that nearer the time though, for now, I had to get a haircut and get to work.

Chapter 6

Into Darkness

It was going to be difficult. I knew what I had to do and the consequences my actions would cause. I'd done similar work before with the NYPD in undercover sting operations but never anything like this, my whole personality would have to change, at least for the foreseeable future. I told Fin what my intention was, he warned me I'd need to go into it full on or I'd mess the whole operation up, but he did tell me he'd have my back, which is what I needed to hear.

Over the weeks, I befriended Kaspar Stahnke, saying the right things at the right time to gain his confidence, the only issue I had was my age. Although in my early fifties, I considered I looked younger, no visible signs of deterioration that you'd expect and with a tight haircut I thought I could pass for a late twenty-something. I got my head shaved by Sam at 'Famous Cutz'. The shop front had signage of a bearded man with a set of scissors designed in a skull and crossbones fashion. Inside, he had it panelled out like a log cabin, it gave warmth to the place, especially in winter. Sam was a nice guy, bald as most barbers are in New York, but always entertaining. To be honest, I enjoyed his company which was why I took the journey over to Midtown, passing by the Empire State Building en route. It was a ten minute walk from the flat, Jody and I would often head out that way when I was due a cut. She'd then go off and leave me with Sam and have a walk around Times Square, maybe do a little shopping. I liked Sam. He kept a good clean shop and exuded confidence in the little swagger he had, it made you feel you were going to get the best damn haircut this side of Manhattan. He also had great people skills, asked the right questions and was a patient guy. I'd seen some kids change their minds halfway through a cut, which must be difficult to adapt to, but he demonstrated his ability and came up with the goods.

None of this stopped him from questioning why I was going so drastic. "A man of your age? It may be a little too harsh for you," he'd said. Sam still believed I was in the Police Department, I hadn't seen him of late and probably hadn't mentioned the fact I'd now got a new job as a private detective.

"I'm going undercover Sam, so make me look twenty years younger." He lifted his scissors in the air and said, "See these, these are scissors man, they ain't a wand."

"Alright, just give it your best shot," I said and settled back into the chair.

I looked in the mirror after the cut and thought, 'Jody's not going to like this, but Sam had achieved the look I needed. I imagined with my old docker's jacket, a pair of Levi's and Doc Marten boots that I kept in the store cupboard from my policing days, I'd cut the look, then Sam showed me a mirror that had a picture of the back of Brad Pitt's head scotch-taped to it.

"Yeah, that's fine, Sam, you'll have to show me how you make me look so good one day, it's genius," I said, smiling.

I thanked him, paid up and said I'd see him when it all grew back again. He gave me his customary farewell. "Adios amigos, until the next time," he said, then spun around on the spot, firing imaginary guns at me, and went to his next customer.

"Oh, Jesus, Gene! What have you done! Did it really need cutting so short?" Jody exclaimed.

"It won't take long to grow back, I just have to get this look right, honey, it's real important," I told her with meaning behind my words.

I'd told Kaspar Stahnke I admired the way he'd set up his websites, giving him an ego boost, but doing so with enthusiasm, saying the right words just when I knew he needed a pat on the back. I told him I was pretty much an amateur with computers but was a fast learner.

He typed, "It's not as easy as just setting a website up, you have to ensure the firewalls keep out the wrong kinda people, Bruno."

I replied, "Well, you know, you've created something to be proud of and I'd like to be a part of it."

The words appeared, "You mean The Radicals? I've been keeping a close eye on you, you seem like the kind of guy who could be useful. We need people like you, people who'll take responsibility for their actions, someone who'll follow through their orders when given, *and* keep the oath of loyalty to the cause."

I replied, "If you point me in the right direction, I'll do the work that's asked of me, and as I said, I learn fast," and then the little dot on the screen paused, no reply came through for several moments, then just when I was about to give up, thinking he'd cut me dead, the little dot started blinking fast, he was typing again.

"Right, I best be able to trust you, because bad things happen to people who let us down," he said.

"I won't let you down, it will be an honour to do something to help the cause," I replied.

"I'll contact you with what we need to do in two days, I need to speak to a few people before we can go any further, it's how we do things. They'll do the checking to find out all about you before anything goes ahead. If you don't check out...," there was another onscreen pause, then a skull and crossbones appeared on screen followed by, "I'll be in touch."

Later, after the exchange, I phoned Emil. I emphasised I was being checked out.

"They could be calling your bluff, but we won't take any chances. I've got a contact. Paulo is first class with computers, but he doesn't come cheap, it'll cost a few bucks. He can do things you wouldn't believe. He helped out in the Schaefer case. He'll give you a 100% foolproof online identity with a past that'll check out and compliment your Six Degrees profile. I'll get him onto it right away and tell him exactly how serious the case is, you'll even get a mobile phone number that will have a history. We've done it before." He hesitated then said, "Late twenties is stretching things more than a bit. Late thirties is better. You could pass for that."

Two days later, Kaspar told me members of the Ultras had to do a test of allegiance. After he told me what it entailed, I really did have doubts, I must admit. I should have known, or at least suspected, that tattoos would be a part of the Radicals. He showed me a photograph of his, a swastika on his forearm. I'd seen it before on the websites he ran. I'd also seen something else on there, which wasn't a tattoo. It looked more like a branding, but he hadn't mentioned that in his post and it played with my mind a little. How far was I prepared to go with this? A tattoo, yes, I could deal with that, they can be removed with a small procedure, but a brand was altogether different, it involved much more pain for a start, which I guess was the point of the ritual. I have to admit it swayed me, for a while I wasn't sure about going through with it, but a chance afternoon with Emil talking about his family changed my mind. I deliberately hadn't told him of the test of loyalty, he'd have advised me not to do it; I just passed on what I thought he could handle, nothing more.

He was telling me about his brother, Filip, and how a Kapo had singled him out and made his life a living hell, his eyes filled with despair as he spoke. Then as the story unravelled, I noticed him watching me, as if for a reaction and I wondered why, but then he told me. He'd killed the Kapo with a spade, and, as he spoke, his eyes searched deep within mine, as if he was looking for absolution.

I was quiet for a few seconds then said, "Emil, you did what any good brother would do, you shouldn't feel any shame." Again, his eyes searched me for forgiveness, so I grabbed hold of his hand, a simple gesture, and he began to weep.

"Such things happened, it was an appalling time, I don't regret killing him, I feel an emptiness, a kind of void, like there's a hole in my soul. I know he deserved what he got, the man was a monstrosity, but to kill carries a terrible burden. Today people kill every day out there on the streets; it seemingly means nothing to them. Life should be more precious than that, it's god's gift and yet it's treated with such disdain by so many people all over the world."

What was I to do? I had to go through with it; my pain would be nothing compared with this man's.

I'd taken on a flat short term whilst I was infiltrating Kaspar's network, these were dangerous people and I couldn't risk my home life with Jody; that just wasn't an option. I'd taken a little squat at $50 a week, it fitted in with who I was portraying and Emil had the bills look like I'd been there for over a year, doctoring some of the mail just in case I was being checked out.

When the day arrived, I met Kaspar and dressed appropriately, the old docker's jacket and DMs would play the part for me. We met at the High Line, the public park situated on the disused elevated railway, he looked dishevelled. It was a deliberate look, his hair was matt black and greasy, he wore a leather jacket and a torn T-shirt, which read, 'The Beaten Generation'. I realised the irony was wasted on Kaspar, I knew the song. It contained the line 'Reared on a diet of prejudice and misinformation. It was by the band 'The The'. He'd obviously just taken the title as a jingoistic term and I doubt he'd ever listened to the lyrics.

"I'm Kaspar, are you Bruno?"

"Yeah," I replied.

"You're thirty-seven. Your Six Degrees profile says you're in the 20 to 30 age group," he questioned. Evidently, he'd checked me out, he knew the age Emil had arranged for me.

"That's right. Vanity got the better of me but would you have allowed me in if I'd have been in the thirty to forty age group?" I replied.

"No, probably not. We're trying to appeal to the younger age group, to give the movement longevity," he said.

I'd done my research on this; these guys were clearly aiming at a younger generation. My age group, or rather the one I was now portraying, was seen as already educated and considered too smart to be radicalised, they wanted the younger more easily led. It was something that America suffered from, a kind of disease, in all shapes and sizes, religion, politics and I'd even seen it in sport.

"Ok, I guess you used initiative and you've shown willing by showing up, so let's go," he said with intent, as he turned and walked off.

After a short walk, we arrived at a small warehouse, it was what Kaspar called his base, untidy with posters of naked women adorning the walls, a sink full of dishes that looked like they'd been there for a week. It was a pigsty.

Our conversation quickly turned to my test of loyalty. "Are you up for it," Kaspar asked, with an enthusiasm I couldn't quite muster myself, but I agreed. I had to gain his trust somehow and if this was how to get it, then I'd just have to suck it up. Emil had gone through things I couldn't even comprehend in his lifetime, so a little pain was nothing in comparison and I kept telling myself that, even as the brand came out of a draw and was placed onto a burner. I could see it was fashioned into a swastika, he looked at me to see if my nerves held.

"It's gonna hurt like hell but you can take it, you're strong and you believe in the cause, don't you?" he said with a smile.

It was then I started talking, just to take my mind off what was about to come, "Do you think I could set up a site like yours, some kind of affiliation subsite? I need to learn from you," I said.

"We'll see, let's just take it one step at a time, I don't know you yet, but I have a good feeling about you. I think you could be someone who could help us, really push the word out and get some following," he replied.

I told him that's exactly what I was aiming at, to get some people in on the mission. "I was drawn to your site, I liked the interview you did with Josef Rösler, I think it's important to have links to the past, it gives the younger generation something to look up to."

"Hell yeah, those guys are heroes of mine, they were actually there, amongst it all. Through my websites, I've had the honour of meeting many great men like him. Baumann, Weiss, Hencke, Von Weber, Schön and more," he said as he took the brand off the gas. "Are you ready, clench your fist tight now," he instructed as he grabbed me by the wrist and placed the brand on my forearm.

"Jesus!!" I screamed but didn't pull away as the burning tore into my arm. For a few seconds, I thought I was going to pass out, but I held firm.

"It hurts like a bastard doesn't it?" Kaspar remarked with a smile.

"Kin A!" I shouted as the searing pain made my heart race, the smell of burning flesh was making me nauseous, especially with it being my own.

"You did well, I've had some that chickened out, they couldn't go through with it, and I'd had to force it on them. You're a true believer now Bruno Lange, you can wear your badge of honor with pride, the pain you feel now, you can use against the enemy."

I shoved my arm beneath the dribble that came from the kitchen faucet. The pain didn't abate for some time and, as I looked at my forearm, thoughts crossed my mind about how I'd ever get it off, somehow I knew I'd have to. I'd crossed the line, my colleagues wouldn't have approved of this. Although I'd informed Fin of my plans, I very much doubt he'd have gone along with getting myself branded like a steer, but I believed I had to do it to get into Kaspar's kinship, to extract the information he had on the people he saw as heroes.

In the build-up to it all, did I hear the name, Baumann? I'd been that preoccupied with the red hot iron bar coming down on me, I hadn't quite caught it, but I was sure he mentioned Baumann. Was he referring to Rudi Baumann? The coincidence was too significant and the question remained, could this neo Nazi who ran an underground network, recruiting followers for the cause, have met *the* Rudi Baumann?

On the strength of what I thought I'd heard, I asked Fin to dig out the Baumann file.

It took a few days for the burn on my arm to settle down, after the initial pain, it had swollen somewhat, which Jody mentioned on the telephone was likely down to an infection. "Idiot of a man," she'd scolded me. I took the pills she'd recommended and noticed a slight improvement.

Fin had gathered the file and read through what we both already knew, a photograph taken in 1943 had been a part of the notes and Fin noted his SS tattoo was visible, The Waffen SS had their blood type tattooed on the underside of the left arm in black ink. The photograph we had was of Baumann in his SS sports vest holding a medicine ball above his head, the Fraktur typeface was visible and Fin told me he'd magnified the photograph several levels.

"You mentioned Darla Platt said the blood type found at Emil's house was of a rare type, can you remember what," he asked me.

"Yes, AB Negative," I told him.

"We've got a match then, Gene. What I'm looking at right here is Baumann's picture during some sports activity, under his left arm his blood group is AB negative. I've run a check, less than one per cent of the American population have that blood group. Coincidences just keep lining up for us my friend," he said.

So, it seemed Rudi Baumann was very much still alive. Could he be a part of this elaborate scheme? If he was, it begged the question, who was the 'Lars' that Saltman had referred to in his interrogation? Amongst the list of heroes, Kasper Stahnke had met was the name Henke and a Forge Ore director was named Lars Henke. There were too many coincidences for them to be simply that. Now we had a probable connection between Baumann and Lars Henke which in turn connected Baumann to Forge and the others.

Fin had been a busy man; he'd also got my recording of Josef Rösler translated and the speech confirmed HIAG were promoting the idealism that the Holocaust hadn't happened at all. They were even advertising in college campus magazines who believed strongly in freedom of speech and civil liberties, which aided Rösler's game plan. He called his statement 'The Holocaust Controversy,' explaining the Jews had died in work camps of disease and claimed they'd tried saving them by creating fumigation chambers where they deloused them. "Yeah, with Zyklon B," I found myself responding aloud.

Emil had been spending a lot of his time with his friend and told me he wouldn't involve him with what we were doing unless he specifically asked to be, he didn't want to put him under any unnecessary stress.

It was a difficult time for me, I couldn't risk anything with Jody, my contact with her and the others was cut back to phone calls from street booths, and even that was a risk. If Kaspar had any doubts about me, the power these people held was frightening. I took no risks and chanced nothing. Kaspar was way down the chain of power, yet I was sure he still had the ability, via his contacts, to cause chaos in my life, so I played it very carefully until I got what I needed from him.

I felt I'd gained his trust, so now I'd gather what information I could and then disappear, it was the reverse of what they'd do in recruiting young, disillusioned people, normally men of a lower educational standing; my plan was based on their own tactics. Emil warned me to be cautious, reminding me about aiming my investigation at Speer. "He has his hands all over this, rumours even circulated in the 60's he was selling stolen art, taken from the victims of the war to subsidise his lifestyle after his release from Spandau," he said.

There was an art dealer I was aware of through the files, one who Speer was linked with. I made a mental note to look his name up when time allowed; I thought there may be something to what Emil was saying.

I sat in the room I'd rented, wishing my budget allowed for a little more luxury, I had very little to do but utilise my downtime thinking about the case. I'd brought along the Speer book, thinking it wouldn't look amiss if Kaspar walked in. I began reading it to fill the time, I was missing Jody, but had to finish the job, I couldn't compromise my position. The pages flowed into one another, and before I knew it, I was halfway through with a little more knowledge about the man. He was certainly the intelligent Nazi, but interaction with people seemed to be his weakness. Although he was considered a charismatic and well-liked member of the Nazi party, like Hitler he had a personality complex, traits that nowadays you'd consider a kind of disorder. I noted that, but concentrated on his intelligence. Was he the man we were seeking? Was he the 'architect' of the final order? Was he the overall architect of the killing centers and gas chambers or was he the 'architect' of the future Fourth Reich? This was the road Emil had me work and concentrate on, it wasn't helpful the man had died some years back, but I could read his own words and interpret them through Emil's eyes; somewhere in between, I might find the real Albert Speer I thought.

A knock came at the door. I answered carefully to find Stahnke standing there. "Kaspar, how did you know where I lived?" I asked, playing it dumb.

"You've been checked out, Bruno. We know everything," he said with menace. I stood wondering what the next move was, and for several moments there was an uncomfortable silence between us. "Are you gonna invite me in," he said.

"Yeah, sure, sorry, I was just surprised to see you, come on in, do you want a beer?" I offered.

"Look, I've had you checked over, to see if we can take this any further. You check out alright, you'll be pleased to hear. It's a good job because I'm warming to you and would've been disappointed to have had to kill you," he said, matter of factly.

"Right, that's a good job then," I said, passing him a Budweiser. "What are you reading?" he asked.

"It's Albert Speer, you know the architect you mentioned?" I said. He looked at me curiously, "I mentioned?" he questioned.

"Yeah, the other week you mentioned in a post about the ultimate betrayal."

"I mentioned?" he repeated, pointing at himself then started laughing. "I wasn't talking about Albert Speer, you idiot. Why would I say Speer betrayed his own, think about it for Christ's sake," he said. "He's the man it was all about, 'The Masterplan,' They set it up for him to take over the Fourth Reich when the time was right. then he died and screwed everything up."

I stood completely confused by it all and didn't want to push any further as I knew I was on the edge of my knowledge. I also didn't want to appear more stupid than I already looked. I changed the subject. "You mentioned all those great men like Weiss, Hencke, Von Weber and others, do you think I'd ever get a chance to interview someone like that? It would be a hell of a scoop," I enquired.

"You'll get the chance, in time," he said.

I pushed further. "I was thinking of setting up a page dedicated to these men, you know, sorta one interview a week, something that would draw people in, get their attention maybe. I don't know, I'm just thinking out loud, trying to find ways to get the word out, you gotta grab the bull by the horns and really get the message across. This country's full of immigrants and we need to take back the control," I said, trying to gain his enthusiasm.

"You're right," he replied, looking around the room, "but we have to do this at the right pace, we've been doing this kind of thing for a long time, it's something we're well practiced at, but I like your enthusiasm." He pointed at my arm. "How's the scar, still hurting like a bastard?" he asked.

"It's not so bad, it's a reminder of what this fight is all about," I replied. "So, who do you know that I could possibly interview, whenever it's right to do so," I asked.

"Do you have any preference?" he replied, teasing me.

"No, I don't know the people you know."

"I know a lot of old Nazi's, they still fight the cause, still have loyalty to the Führer, and are all still good men," he said.

I nodded understanding. "It's just if I'm going to interview someone, I should at least do my homework, so I don't ask a stupid god damn question."

"Yeah, I get that, but we aren't at that stage yet. I'll let you know when there's clearance, your enthusiasm is noted and I'll pass it on to those who make the decisions." With that, he took another glance around and left; he'd be in touch.

Yeah, I was enthusiastic, mainly to get the information I needed and get the hell out of this shit hole, get back to my own life, I was beginning to feel a part of this flat and its very distinctive style. I went back to the book and gave it a couple of hours for Stahnke or any of his friends who might be watching the place to get bored and go home before I called Emil to update him. I also called Jody and told her I missed her.

I decided my next meeting with Kaspar Stahnke would be the one I pushed him about meaningful contact. I couldn't keep this up for much longer, I didn't like the people I was dealing with, in fact, I hated them and they made my skin crawl.

I had it all planned out, next time, he'd either tell me or I'd beat the living crap out of him until he did. I was getting the names I needed from Kaspar Stahnke, willingly or not.

Chapter 7

The New Order

Kaspar was good to his word, a week later he told me he'd passed a message down the line with regard to an interview for the 'The Ultras,' website. He'd told them 'Bruno Lange' was a bright new radical, who'd passed his initiation test with honor, and it would be beneficial to the movement to enthuse him, show him who the real Nazis are, whoever *they* were. It was arranged. I'd have to study up on Rudi Baumann, get to know the things that were familiar to others. More importantly, I needed to try and forget the things I already knew about him, that would be a dead giveaway letting slip something trivial, it would emphasise I'd been reading the wrong kind of information, according to them. In fairness, I just wanted to get home to a hot bath and a meal, sit with Jody by the fire and relax, the simple things in life. I'd been undercover on this case for over a month now, it was the longest time we'd spent apart, and it became evident. She'd say things when I called, things which made me know she was trying to make light of the situation but wasn't feeling it in reality. I'd reassure her that it was just this one part of the job that had to be done. "It won't always be like this," I'd told her, 'I'm using a fish to catch a whale,' but again as soon as the words came out, they all seemed wrong.

I'd never really known Jody upset before, I guess deep down she was worried for me, the image I'd taken on board and the injury had all happened relatively quickly. The transition from the NYPD day job to the work I now found myself in happened way too fast for her, I think, but personally, I enjoyed it, for the most part, it was real work, and we were tracking down legitimate criminals. I suppose you could say I got satisfaction from the work, more than I'd ever gotten working on homicide, that to me was just a paycheck and it hadn't always been pleasant work, but there was just something about this that made me feel proud of what we were doing, and then there was Emil, who I'd taken on board as a kind of father figure, I just couldn't let him down. I'd sort things out with Jody, she was a strong woman, I loved her and that would pull us through all of this, but it'd been particularly hard for her, this separation, and I hadn't realised. I guess her routine had been completely messed up by me, maybe she enjoyed her days just the way they were thank you very much, and here I was throwing her whole life out of kilter. I told her each call that I loved her and that I'd make it up to her when I grew my hair back. Once, I even said I'd grow a ponytail just to lighten the mood a little. It made her laugh through her tears, "You look like a thug, I don't like to see you that way, it's not who you are, but I understand, it's just something you have to do, but I'm afraid," she'd said, then quickly changed the subject, "I think Emil's very proud of you, he phones me every evening to see how I'm coping without you. He speaks of you with a great fondness, like a son or brother and even calls you Filip now and then," she told me.

Although life like this was difficult, I knew I was close. All I needed was a location to meet Baumann, Fin and I would sort the rest out.

Stahnke arranged the meeting with Baumann at a place that was not too far from the Flat Iron building, which was a major concern for me. I had a moment of panic, thinking he might be sending me a message, but it wasn't just that. It was a little too close for comfort because I'd often take walks with Jody in Tomkins

Square Park; I might meet someone I knew. But, I didn't have a choice in the matter; the meeting was arranged on their terms.

I prepared myself. I thought about the message left at Idar Court when Max had been shot, it was more than likely Baumann who'd left it. Ilse Gerver wouldn't be on my questions list that was for sure. One slip up and the whole deck of cards would collapse, and I couldn't risk that. I briefed Emil and Fin and we agreed I'd go it alone; it was too risky to have someone tailing me up close, and being wired was a death sentence. Fin would stay in the background at a distance watching. It was me that set this all up, so it was my head on the chopping block and in a strange way I wanted to test myself, after all, that's the reason I'd applied for the job in the first place. Anyway, I'd learned to channel my hatred and use it as a strength; to assist me with all the lies I'd be telling.

The day of the interview came quickly. I'd rehearsed my questions, nothing too personal, just enough to inspire the idealism. Kaspar had told me of 'The New Order,' an all-new Germany imposing its will on the conquered areas under its new dominion. He'd spoken of it with great enthusiasm, with crazed eyes, words that fifty years ago would have had great sway on the general public, but in a modern world sounded shallow and quite crazy.

"We'll take it piece by piece, town by town and city by city, if necessary, until there is a new world order," he'd announced to me. But he was just a small part of a big wheel, the centre of which had the potential to make Kaspar's words a frightening reality. That's what I was aiming at, whatever was powering the hub which turned the wheel.

I spoke with Fin from a call booth to get reassurances he somehow had my back covered, his words gave me comfort, but he had other news, something interesting he said. "I was digging around looking for information about Vaschel Saltman and more so his father Rudy who was killed in the liberation of Auschwitz, as you know, I came across some photographs of the inmates, I'm pretty sure one of them is Emil," he said.

"Jesus, Fin, don't say anything to him, and certainly don't show him the photograph, it'd break the guy," I told him.

"No, let me finish, the picture has him with two other men, one older than him with a resemblance, it could well be his father, but the other..." he paused whilst thinking before he told me, "The other has a resemblance," he paused.

"To who?" I asked, genuinely intrigued.

"He looks identical to you," he said with certainty about his words.

"What do you mean me?" I responded.

"Gene, the photograph has the image of you standing next to a younger and somewhat malnourished Emil Janowitz, it's definitely him. The photographs have a name at the bottom, a Wilhelm Brasse, who I'm assuming is the photographer, it looks like it was published in the New York Times in 1958. I'm telling you, Gene, this guy is uncannily like you, you're like two peas in a pod and I'm wondering if Emil has seen this before. Don't worry, I won't show him, but again the coincidences just keep stacking up here, why you and why now," he said, and a chill ran down my spine as if someone had just walked across my grave.

Unaware, Fin just carried on. "There's two photographs, one he's standing with other inmates, and it looks a lot later than the other, as he's lost a lot more weight, and this one I have here with the two men, which looks like it's at the entry gates to Auschwitz. I'm not sure if he's working, or just entered the camp. The other photograph shows in more detail a group of men all looking close to death's door, their eyes are drawn back into their heads, knee bones protruding out with no flesh around them. Jesus, it's an awful scene. Anyway, I thought you needed to know I've found your doppelgänger," he said.

The conversation had disturbed me a little, I don't know why but it just seemed strange, after all, Emil had recently told me about seeing his brother within people he saw on the streets, so I thought about it for a while, then put it out of my mind and concentrated on the job at hand.

Rudi Baumann had been SS at Belsen concentration camp; we knew of a close relationship with Ilse Gerver but the exact nature wasn't apparent. Older now, in his late seventies, he approached us in Tomkins Square Park. He still looked like a formidable man and greeted Kaspar with a handshake then turned to me. "So, you're Bruno Lange? Kaspar has told me all about you, he speaks highly of your enthusiasm," he said. I noted his eyes were black and deep-set, giving me the impression of evil hidden within. He reminded me of a shark, nothing behind the eyes but death.

"Come, we should walk," he told me. Momentarily, I couldn't believe I was walking alongside a real-life Nazi and almost forgot the reason why.

I wasn't aware of him being sought by the authorities anywhere and, it appeared, neither was he because when I asked him if it was ok to film he surprisingly said yes. Clicking into action, I introduced myself to camera, giving a little pre-rehearsed speech then introduced him and sprang into my questioning,

"Can you tell me what it was like back then, the feelings you had..." but before I could finish, he started to reply.

"We had power, immense power back then, you have no idea how strong we were, we had the world at our feet and it was amazing. We could have done anything, our idealism was to have a thousand years Reich but it could have been much more," he replied, with passion.

I asked him several more questions, nothing too probing because I wanted to keep their trust and, after all, it was destined for the Ultras' website for the purposes of a Neo-Fascist recruitment campaign. He surprised me by not denying the 'Holocaust'. He simply maintained that for a new world order you had to eliminate and sweep away the old.

"The day will come when we will rise like the phoenix from the flame, out of the ashes we will conquer and rule," he'd menacingly said. He may have sounded crazy to some but he had an intensity about him that chilled me to the bone.

I thanked him for his time, knowing when he left, Fin would be tailing him back to the stone he'd crawled out from under. It had been the main purpose of the whole thing; this was the strategy, find, locate and wait until the time was right.

Fin worked solidly on Baumann, whilst I took a back seat maintaining contact with Stahnke periodically over the next few weeks. He kept me up to scratch with the comings and goings around Baumann, who seemed a popular old man amongst a certain crowd.

He was a smart guy, Fin. He used a few of his old buddies for the surveillance, he knew how to use modern technology and his skills at picking locks had helped gain entry to the apartment in Greenwich that Baumann temporarily called home. That was a break for us, finding him so close to home. Once in, Fin placed several pinhole cameras and bugged the phone with something so small you just wouldn't have realised what it was if you put it in your hand.

Technology had come a long way and he was able to place a little known programme of forensic intelligence software on the laptop Baumann used. It worked a bit like a virus and gave us access to everything, apart from a couple of encrypted files we'd have to work on later. It didn't matter if the thing was turned off, we could still get in. The stuff had been developed through the military and was used by their intelligence agencies. When I asked him how he'd got it he just shrugged his shoulders and tapped his nose. It was good to have contacts.

Baumann apparently didn't have friends in the military so although he had security on his computer it was no match for what Fin was using. We got some very interesting stuff and Fin knew a guy who knew a guy who knew the guy that was a former top hacker now working for the FBI. On the promise that if he found anything the Feds could use he got the kudos, he went to work. Company emails, client to client, contacts with the other directors, brokers working in other countries and for multinationals. We learned that Forge had been financed a long time ago through investments far and wide in companies old and new. The likes of BASF and Bayer which had formed part of IG Farben and re-emerged when it was broken back down to its constituent parts particularly caught Fin's guy's attention. It looked like insider trading had also played a part, and that it still was. He managed to locate their database, gain entry and whilst tracking some transactions came up with the surprising information that subsidiaries of Forge were funding far-left and anarchist groups. It took us quite a while before we figured that one out, and at this point we were clueless.

But the most immediately interesting matters were that Baumann's car had outstanding parking violations in Greenwich, he wasn't a United States citizen and, surprise surprise, he was in the country illegally.

Why hadn't anyone caught up with him? It was simple. Although *we* knew he existed and who he was, no one else did. Nothing was in his name; his apartment was leased by a company that turned out to be front for Forge's interests under a no mark name only slightly more inventive than John Doe. Still, the parking violations were going to come in handy in the short term.

Tapped telephone calls confirmed the connection Baumann had with Forge Ore and the one from Otto Weiss, whilst disclosing nothing more than extreme displeasure for the Ultras interview, had established Weiss was still on the planet, although exactly where we weren't sure.

From what Emil had told us, up to 73 tons of gold plundered from those murdered in the camps and elsewhere had gone missing after the war. Even though Venezuela had taken its share as protection for the former Nazi's, we figured there would still have been an awful lot left.

"Can you imagine how much that amount of gold is worth in today's market?" Fin asked.

I told him Jody had just sold some of her old jewellery and we knew it was trading at $380 an ounce. "I guess it's gone tenfold since the war," I said.

"So, Gene, we are talking around $11 million a ton, then multiply that by a possible 73," he was working it out in his head. "How does that add up?" he suddenly asked.

"Jesus, Fin I don't know, you lost me when you started counting, let's just say it's a hell of a lot of money," I offered him back.

He came back with, "Yeah, sure, I'd suggest over a billion dollars now that's a hell of a lot of money. If they've been selling this stuff off since 1974 and investing in shares in companies, Jesus, this could be one hell of a sized company. I'm talking about the wealth of a small well-developed country." He shook his head then spoke in Gaelic, "Nách mór an diabhal thú." He saw my blank look and explained, "It means, now aren't you the devil." He meant Forge and I nodded in agreement.

All this time, I still had some contact with Kaspar Stahnke. I'd told him I was working on my own website and he wanted to know how I was doing, why hadn't I got it up and running yet so we could make the affiliation links. He offered to help me but I said I wanted to do it myself because I needed to learn, but if it got too difficult I'd let him know. In his next posts to me, he got talkative, telling me how he knew where Nazi gold was hidden. First, it was beneath a 16th-century Hochberg Palace in the village of Roztoka, Poland, then he spoke of the Wałbrzych gold train that was allegedly hidden by the Nazis in the 'Owl Mountains' during the last days of the war. He was starting to ramble and I got the impression he'd been drinking. I felt he was under pressure from somewhere.

We discussed it and decided it was time Baumann was arrested. It was a two-fold thing. We hoped we could persuade him to co-operate *and* put Stahnke under even more pressure at the same time. Emil's contact in the local Police, his old boss Cooper Collins, was happy to assist and made the arrest himself. He allowed us to take part in the interview.

I walked into the interview room, the sort of room I'd been in a thousand times. Before I could introduce myself or give any acknowledgement to Baumann, he made the first move. "You're a liar, Bruno Lange, you betrayed us," he said.

"My name is Eugene Kennedy, Mr Baumann, let's get that straight from the get-go." Fin pushed the tape machine's record button and I began. "I'd like to ask you a little about Ilse Gerver."

"You bastard, I'll kill you." He lunged forward, across the desk, Fin pushed him back in his seat.

"Good, I'll take that as you're familiar with the lady and our involvement with her, Mr Baumann."

He leaned slowly forward and whispered, "We're going to kill every member of your family."

"Now, that's not very nice, Rudi. But thanks for confirming your associations. Back to Ilse."

"You killed her. You are responsible for her death," he replied.

I ignored it. "You two had a special bond, I think, Rudi. Tell us about it?"

"It is none of your business. I want to call my lawyer and then I shall pay off these ridiculous fines." He smirked at me, I wanted to punch him but didn't.

I looked up at Cooper. "Didn't you tell him?"

He shook his head. "I guess in all the excitement, I forgot."

We had Baumann's full attention; he didn't look quite so sure of himself anymore. "Tell me what?"

I gave him my most innocent smile. "Oh, just a little matter, some nice people from Immigration would like to speak to you about and when they've finished..." I shot a glance at Cooper who nodded back. "Yeah, when they've finished there's a prosecutor in Germany with a big file and they're very keen to speak to you. They've been searching for you for a long time now."

The look on Baumann's face was the only real benefit we got from that interview. He wasn't telling us anything. We asked the questions and he denied knowledge, even claiming that his associations with the Forge Ore people were purely coincidental, they were simply members of an American German friendly society. We knew it was a lie, another front of Forge's. When the tape was turned off he said, "You will pay the price for this. You've no idea the sort of people you are dealing with."

It was disappointing but we had to live with it and decided to move on to Stahnke. We weren't sure how much he really knew and, as Cooper Collins pointed out, he hadn't actually committed any offenses he could be arrested for.

I don't know what happened next but it was almost as if he read Fin's mind. He excused himself then left and that's when Fin suggested we break into Kaspar's place and download his computer. I was given the job of arranging a 'meet' to get him out of the way.

So, there I was, in a burger bar three blocks from his warehouse apartment. He seemed distracted and nervous. I played him with the need for me to interview another of his 'names' and tried to string the conversation out. He half-heartedly said he'd see what he could do but when he suddenly got up to leave all I could think of to delay him was to give him my mobile number, Emil had bought us all the new Nokia 232 which was a damn sight smaller than the previous alternatives. It didn't delay him long and, as soon as he was out of the door, I called Fin. "He's on his way back, I couldn't keep him any longer."

"Fuck! Gene, I give you one simple job," was all he replied.

We met up back at Emil's, I was the last to get there and that's when Fin broke the news. "I had to take his computer. He had a load of 'floppys' and just didn't have time to view them so decided to take everything."

"Gee, Fin. Do you think he might notice?" I replied.

Stahnke called me within two hours. "I don't know who the fuck you are, Bruno Lange, but you just signed my death warrant."

I tried to bullshit him, deny knowledge, but he knew. "What are you? Government or freelancer? You dumbshit! You just killed me, Bruno! They're gonna get me, you sonofabitch!"

"Kaspar, we can help you. Come in from the cold. We're not Government, we're much better than that. We have the resources." The phone went dead.

Another two hours and he called again. "You gotta help me. I want to come in."

We took him to a motel, a temporary haven whilst Emil took care of finding us a safe house.

"You're just a little cog in a big machine, Kaspar, one that's been used. I can see that. I got close to you so I know deep down who you are, we're not so far apart you and I, this Nazi shit aside, but you knew you were playing with bad people and now you have an opportunity to help yourself and send them down at the same time. Give me a name, Kaspar, and I'll tell you what they really did, not the sanitised crap they've been telling you."

"I can't, I just can't," he whined.

Fin stood up. "Alright, Geno, let's get the hell out of here we're wasting our time with this fool. Hell, once we get through his computer security, and we will, we won't need him at all."

I got up also but watched Kaspar's reaction, he sat shaking his head from side to side as if asking himself the big question. "Alright, if I give you a name...," he started but Fin interrupted. "No son, you tell us everything you know, every last god damn thing or there's no deal."

Kaspar Stahnke folded like a pack of cards, offering names already on our list and a few that weren't but with his knowledge we could cut corners. He gave us information that would allow us to draw our picture a lot more accurately.

I thought I'd ask him about Speer, Emil was still keen on his theory. Kaspar said he'd looked up to him as being the next Führer but also said Speer was his own man; upon being questioned about becoming the new leader of the Neo Nazis, he'd said no. An aspiration he'd once had was no more, once he'd realised the potential of the life he'd now assumed. His refusal was done in his usual polite manner so as to keep everyone onside and then at the age of 76 he'd died of a heart attack, in London, of all places.

Rightly or wrongly, Emil wanted Speer's name associated with Auschwitz and the Holocaust. He believed with every bone in his body that it had to be Speer who gave the 'Final Order'. He'd taken Kaspar Stahnke's words about 'The Architect' as the incentive to light the blue touch paper, and that had been my fault. It was me who'd told him and I felt some guilt. I didn't want to see the light go out in Emil's eyes, his enthusiasm was infectious, both Fin and I fed off it and we became better at our jobs because of it.

"Tell me about The Architect," I asked, not really knowing where we were going or what would come from it all.

"What is it you want? A name? That's it isn't it, you don't know who he is, do you? Jesus, you guys haven't a god damn clue have you, ok let's take a wander down that road shall we," he said.

We were silent for a moment then he spoke. "The Lazarus Project, I know all about it, who's involved, people working on it past and present, and that's just one of their projects."

I'd read something in the files about this, it was a so-called conspiracy theory, the idea was when the SS had their blood group tattooed on their arm a blood sample was taken at the same time, taken away and stored at a secret location in a cold store, 'The Lazarus Project,' had been Hitler's idea they said, some thought it pure fantasy, dreamt up after the war, others convinced of its existence after they'd found out what the Nazi's had been doing concerning eugenics and the like. Some facts, some fiction the file had it noted under 'Reality??'

"You've gotta do better than that, Kaspar. I can pick up a story like that on 'Dark Skies'," I told him.

"No, you can't. I can give you information that's solid, names, addresses, hospitals. Do you know what I mean?" He looked at me searchingly. "Yeah, I think you're a decent man underneath. I need some assurances. Legal stuff, in writing. I want a new identity, one that stands up to scrutiny, like the stuff you had. I know you can do it. And I want money. I know you'll crack my computer's security but then you'll have to crack the encryptions I've got on all the really good stuff. It could take you months, I reckon. It *will* take you months unless I give you the clues you'll need. In that time, those you're after will have disappeared into the mist. What do you say, Geno?"

I knew he was right and we couldn't afford to waste the time. "How much money are you asking for?"

"$500,000. I'm not greedy."

"$200,000 or nothing." I'd break the news to Emil later but I knew he was more than good for it, sometimes you have to think on your feet. I caught Fin's eye. He nodded acceptance.

When I told Emil about 'The Lazarus Project,' he looked at me straight in the eye. "You know this is a film don't you?"

I hadn't seen 'The Boys from Brazil,' so he filled me in on the basic idea.

"So, are you saying it's Hitler's blood he's trying to negotiate with, his DNA?" I asked.

"The boy wants to engage your mind. Even I know Hitler's dead. These are dreams of the Neo Nazi's believing in the resurrection of their Christ figure. It's pure fantasy, Eugene, and you should treat it that way," he told me. "I'm not convinced about Speer. He's hiding him behind this mask of the 'Lazarus Project,' the boy knows he has you hooked, he's playing with your mind, however, you can use that, accept it, draw up some paperwork, gain his confidence. You asked him about 'The Architect' and he sidestepped it. Get the encryption key from him. Get him back on track."

We drank a few beers and I walked him back home, he was greeted as usual on the doorstep by Luiza. I stayed and had Sunday lunch with them both but we never brought the subject up in front of Luiza, it was her day with her husband.

After the meal, we sat out in the garden. Emil had made a beautiful friendly space that Luiza loved, enjoying a glass of wine at night, sitting out listening to nature all around her. She hand-fed the birds; I was amazed at their gentleness; they trusted her. "Here you try it," she said to me.

I knelt and put my hand out, at first nothing happened, then one little bird was brave enough to hop towards me, gathering together his trust, he flew up into my hand and pecked away at the seeds, it was relaxing I must admit. I don't know but after the chaos of the last weeks, it just felt so easy, I could have lain down on the lawn and allowed the birds to accept me. "You're a natural," Luiza commented.

Then I noticed a small bird with brilliant colours on its chest, yellow with brilliant red wings, I'd not seen one like it before. When it noticed me it flew off up into the trees, watching over as the other birds fed.

I stayed over that night, a little drunk on red wine. I guess the workload had caught up on me and I'd fallen asleep in the garden on Emil's steamer chair. It was Luiza who woke me, telling me she'd made a bed up. "It's too late to go home, Eugene, you're tired." She was insistent. I phoned Jody and apologised.

Emil came out and said, "You've been overdoing it lately, one bottle of wine wouldn't make you like this, you're exhausted, Eugene," he said.

Before I could answer, Luiza had my arm and I was being escorted to my bed, "Thanks, Luiza, you're a diamond," I said to her as she closed the bedroom door.

The little red bird remained with me as I fell into a deep sleep, once again I found myself in the grounds of

Auschwitz, this time I was watching a cart with bodies on it being taken away. I felt great emotion, I didn't know why but as I looked up to a window ledge I saw the bird watching over, just like Emil had described to me. It looked directly at me and flew off. I noticed my skin was emaciated and it frightened me, I was just skin and bones, a gong rang for roll call and I woke with a start. It was morning and Luiza had placed a cup of tea next to me and the spoon had fallen to the wooden floor.

We went back to Stahnke. Fin's buddies had babysat; we didn't want Kaspar making a dash for Wyoming or somewhere else big and lonely. I told him we'd agreed to his terms. Then I asked him what he'd meant when he'd said, 'The ultimate betrayal is of your own kind, and nobody betrayed their own more so than the Architect'. I told him I wanted a name this time.

He smiled. "The Architect I spoke of was at Auschwitz and Bełżec. Look for Jonah Silverman."

"Why was he called the Architect?" Fin asked.

"Because he designed things."

"What sort of things."

"Look, I don't know for certain. I heard these guys talking together when I met them for the Ultras' site. They were laughing and saying how ironic it was that a Jew had designed the gas chambers. That's what I meant about the ultimate betrayal."

We pushed him on his encryption key but he wanted his documents, agreement and money first. Fin wanted to shortcut things and beat the information out of him but it wasn't the way I wanted to go. We needed to check what he'd told us first, I told him.

I decided to dig deep on this one and found a New York Times report concerning the designer of the Auschwitz gas chambers and crematoria being acquitted in an Austrian court, The name given was Walter Dejaco. It seemed he'd taken credit for the work amongst the SS and all the blueprints bore his signature but he maintained he hadn't drawn them up and had never visited the site of the installations. I found another report which described Himmler's special visit to see the new crematoria in action for the first time. They chose 3,000 Polish Jews to have the 'honor' of demonstrating its efficiency.

Could Stahnke's story be true, it was someone else who designed them, an inmate, perhaps a Jew?

Our information indicated that the designer of the gas chambers had 'cut his teeth' on Bełżec's. To get any confirmation we'd need to find someone who'd been an inmate at the relevant time and we weren't hopeful because records showed us that only 7 people were believed to have survived Bełżec at war's end and, at the moment, all we were coming up with was dead people. Fin discovered, however, that Jonah Silverman was alive and seemingly well, living in the outskirts of Mendoza, Chile. He hadn't even changed his name, apparently not a care in the world.

Silverman had entered Auschwitz concentration camp in the spring of 1940, endearing himself to the camp hierarchy with his knowledge of construction and numeracy skills. He was a young man then, almost still a boy, and a non-Orthodox Jew. It looked like he went on to assist the design and construction of Bełżec concentration camp and the gas chambers of Birkenau. It was all there in the archived documents, his name was on the sheets of those involved in the construction.

When we told him our news, Emil idly said, "Lars worked in the construction at Bełżec."

We went back to Stahnke and let him know what he was telling us was checking out.

"So, we have a deal," he said.

"Yeah, we'd have drawn up the papers but someone strangled our lawyer and dumped him in the Hudson. We're finding a replacement," I told him.

He just replied, "You know these people will kill you, all if you're not clever, not only that but your families and friends too. They'll stop at nothing to protect what they have, to protect the future of the Fourth Reich, they're still in a war and you're the enemy, so don't expect a welcome committee. Leon Spiel was killed for what he knew, they realised using him was a mistake and he'd eventually give up a name, so it was simple, they stopped that happening."

Fin had been working on Stahnke's files and had some success with a couple of items that were low grade encrypted but not currently of interest to us, we knew he was holding out until we produced the goods but, anxious to access higher grade stuff, Fin came up with the idea of giving Kaspar a 'party' to thank him for his co-operation and get him drunk. We had a party of three, no girls, no dancing, just beer and bourbon.

We judged by looking at him that he wasn't the world's greatest drinker and were right. Several beers and bourbons later he'd passed through the cautious and serious phases and was now just plain happy and cocky.

"Do you know how cunning these people are? You wouldn't believe what I'm going to tell you. They're actually funding left-wing extremists and anarchists." He sat back with a smirk on his face. We believed him, we already knew but hadn't worked out why.

I adopted an incredulous look as if this was the first time I'd heard. "What! How the hell does that work for them?"

He held his glass out for another slug of bourbon. "It's just two legs on the same body, Geno. Extreme left and right, it's there to see if you bother looking. Why do you think Hitler changed the name of the Party to the National *Socialists* Workers Party? It captured thousands of new members, some of whom had been communists. Do you think they are keen on the Jews? You'd be a fool if you did. They see them as being rich and part of the ruling classes."

"So where do they go from there?" Fin added.

"This is a long term plan. The left and anarchists are the real 'New Radicals'. The 'Ultras' and the like are just a distraction intended to attract attention whilst the extreme left renew, reorganise and regenerate, they've been infiltrated by our people already. The mistake made is thinking the animosity between the Communists and the Nazis was all about ideology. Bullshit it was! All that crap was just something to fool the masses. It was about competition for power, the ultimate power." He took another slug from his glass."You wait and see, it'll happen in the next twenty years if not sooner. Who fucking cares what uniform they're wearing when the time comes. Money and power, that's what the Fourth Reich is all about. It's fucking genius."

Fin exchanged a glance with me and a smile then popped a beer for Kaspar who had decided he was on a roll.

"Do you know how I know so much?"

Did we want to know how he knew so much stuff? Yeah, sure. He said he was a hacker. No, we didn't believe him. That sort of annoyed him a bit so he went on to tell us what he knew and how he'd found it all out.

"I'm a Hacker," he declared again. "My talent isn't just about building websites, that sort of work is for the paycheck. I go by the name of 'The Innominate'. Do you have any idea what a hacker does?" he asked.

"Enlighten me, Kaspar," I replied.

"If I was to tell you the FBI have me on their top twenty wanted list would that assist you?"

"Go on, we're listening," I responded.

"I'm wanted on several counts of breaking into various computer systems, Government Agencies, Jewish organisations, I even hacked the Israeli Defence Force. Sometimes, I just get in and cause as much chaos as possible. Hell, I once sent an email that had every computer on a network print off hundreds of sheets of paper in black ink."

"So, you just fool around, nothing serious then?" I said.

He laughed. "How do you think I know so much about their plans? I didn't just listen carefully to their conversations when I was in their company and I can get into anything. My allegiances might be to the forthcoming Reich but I'm a Hacker at heart who wants to find out anything about everything, *that's* why I know everything. Your Architect was a protégé and confidant of Albert Speer who was Adolf Hitler's right-hand man. Did you know the Führer wanted to pass the armband to Speer? *He* was the chosen one, the man trusted to take Germany forward and he could have done, had they not conspired against him. That's why he gave his evidence at Nuremberg the way he did."

Fin interrupted, "That and plain old self-preservation."

Stahnke wasn't listening. Filling his glass with more bourbon from the 'Evan Williams' bottle, he stood upright, raised his hand and downed the drink in one before saying, "Sich erneuern, Sich neu bilden, Sich regenerieren... renew, reorganise and regenerate, that's how to create the Fourth Reich." He then promptly slumped onto the couch, tried to stand up again then gave up.

Fin and I realised we'd misjudged him. He could take less alcohol than even we thought.

"Who gave the Final Order, Kaspar," I asked him, quietly.

"I don't know that, but I know a man who will," he slurred with a smile. We assumed he meant Silverman.

We decided to let him sleep it off and left him with the babysitters, heading to a nearby bar to regroup our thoughts.

"So, what do you think?" Fin said as he put a couple of beers on the table.

"I think he's right. That's what this is about now, power and money, not really ideology, they'll sort out what uniform they wear out later. Hitler did it in 1933, building the numbers up to a point where they couldn't be resisted anymore by the ordinary people, then when the Socialist elements and others began to agitate – Bam! Along comes 'night of the long knives'. They cut the head off the increasingly unruly organised mob they'd created and brought everyone to heel. It's a long term strategy and these old guys probably won't see it to fruition but I'd suggest they have enough ardent followers to carry this through."

"But what about the far-right activists?"

"Apart from Stahnke, I don't suppose they know. I think the hierarchy realised that pushing their boat out into the mainstream isn't going to work. Anyone with a sound mind hates the Nazis, you just have to say the word and then say 'Communist'. The effects on the brain aren't the same. Hell, you could almost cuddle a communist in comparison." I took a mouthful of beer. "Do you know what? I think it's time to speak to the Feds."

"That's me," he said as he stood up and checked his mobile and took the call outside. When he returned he gave me a big grin and said, "We don't need Kaspar anymore. My guy's got in. The ciphers are broken and he's looking at a lot of *very* interesting stuff."

Over a glass of wine that night, whilst Jody was watching one of her favourite shows, I started thinking about something Stahnke had said in interview which I'd taken as bullshit; The Lazarus Project

I asked her because if anyone would know I figured she would, "Can you really copy a whole person's DNA into somebody else?"

I was distracting her, I know, so I didn't have her full attention but she'd seen this particular show before. She told me in theory it was possible to take just one single cell from a person and in laboratory conditions make a carbon copy of the host body it was taken from. It seems no one had done it yet but there was a team in England working on it and they felt they were close to achieving it. It was food for thought but I wasn't finished.

When Emil's dog, Max, was shot, Darla Platt, the CSI on the case, took samples at the crime scene, she tested for blood and found a rare group, the one that matched Baumann's. She'd also told me, there was confusing data with another sample she'd found which showed two DNA strains. She'd ignored it believing the sample up had somehow got messed up, so now I had another question. "Jody, can someone have two different DNAs in their body?" She replied, absently, "It's possible. For instance, a woman can retain the DNA of her baby or it can happen when a foetus absorbs a twin and it can happen when you have a bone marrow transplant, in that situation the donors marrow continues making blood cells that have their DNA."

The next day, I let the others know what she'd told me. Fin's response was, "Walt Disney." It didn't hit home.

"No idea Fin, what the hell do you mean, Walt Disney?"

"Don't you know the story about him being cryogenically frozen?" he said.

"No, but I'm still at a loss, what the hell's that to do with DNA?"

"Well, he had money and was interested in cryogenics apparently. I read a book about him that claims, at his request, they had his body frozen so he could wait out advances in technology and maybe come back someday," he replied.

I'd not really heard any of this and could only take Fin's word for it but then again this was a guy who liked to read Marvel Comics superhero magazines. I think what I got out of that conversation was confusion, so I decided not to mention the DNA again.

Later that night, I told Emil about my dreams and he told me they were very similar to his own. "It must be the consequence of the work," he simply concluded. I wasn't so sure.

Chapter 8

The Money Trail

We now had evidence that the Nazi's had been funnelling money through America via financial institutions, shares in companies and the top-performing stocks: agriculture, animal stock, coffee, butter, fruit, sugar, plastics, natural gas and biofuels. In fact, they had fingers in more pies than we could check on, but it was the precious metals we had eyes for.

After the war, IG Farben, the company that made Zyklon B which was used to kill people in the gas chambers, was found to hold an account within Chile, in the same bank as the former Nazi's we were investigating.

They'd helped set up weapons factories there making Sarin gas with former IG Farben scientists overseeing the process. Ostensibly for the use of the Chileans, we believed its real purpose was connected to the initial plans for the Reich to go back to war. It looked like Kaspar Stahnke was right, it was big, much bigger than we'd ever imagined.

I walked in on Fin and Emil one day and asked, "Anyone heard of the BIS?"

Fin shook his head, "What's it stand for?"

Emil answered, "The Bank for International Settlements."

"That's right!" I replied. "What do you know, Emil?"

He smiled, "Tell me what you know, first."

So I did, trotting it out like I was giving a presentation at school. "The Bank for International Settlements was set up to facilitate reparations imposed on Germany after World War One. Its members were the interested parties, Belgium, Germany, Britain, France, Italy, Japan, the USA and, of course, Switzerland who just likes anything to do with money. The interesting thing is that during World War Two, when its president was an American guy called McKittrick, *whilst* these countries were at war with each other, apart from Switzerland who just held the money, the heads of their national banks continued to meet as if nothing was going on. For them, it was business as usual and they liked doing business. The gold stolen from the Jews of Europe was deposited in Switzerland and managed through the BIS."

Fin was incredulous. "Hey, I know, during the war, Hoover had the Feds close down a bank that George Bush's daddy was heavily involved in for 'trading with the enemy' because they'd been managing Nazi money and they knew it was Nazi money. But how could this thing be going on? You're saying whilst everyone else is fighting, these people were filling their pockets?"

"It's worse than that," I replied. "Basically, they laundered the stolen gold. Swiss banks still keep a lot and won't return it because they say they don't know who the owners are."

Emil let an ironic little smile wander across his face. "It's true. The gold was melted down and remade into ingots so, technically, they are correct, morally, that's another matter."

"So, what do you know about all this?" I asked him.

"You've given a good account, Eugene. I presume you found this because you were looking for another way that Schröder and his friends could have got their money. I suspect, like you have, that a German submarine can't carry that much gold. How do I know about them? I came across the BIS through Aleksy's files. Those people should have been shot or at least imprisoned for their treachery but they weren't!"

I couldn't help asking, "But why not?".

"Because, Eugene, money makes the world go round. Someone wrote a song about it, I thought you might have heard it."

Fin interrupted, "So how did they get the gold to South America? On a big ship?"

Another little smile from Emil. "It's possible, but such a thing could attract too much attention, especially at that time, and what if the ship sinks, they have a tendency to do that. No, Fin, in its simplest form, the gold is deposited in Swiss banks and is managed by the BIS who issue 'loans' to the 'owners'. Now these 'owners' aren't going to pay the money back so the Swiss banks keep the equivalent gold and the BIS takes its commission. If the Nazis want to pay for acceptance in another country they have gold transferred to that country's account in Switzerland and then that country prints more money. The Nazis wander into wherever they have their local accounts and take *their* money out. It can be a bit more complex, but you get the gist."

We sat in silence for a while, then Emil said, "The head of the German's Reichsbank sat on the board of the Bank for International Settlements, the head of the Bank of England also. For a while, the German representative was a man called Walter Funk who in 1941 launched a plan which he named the 'Europaische Wirtschafts Gemeinschaft'. In English, that means the 'European Economic Community'. For all intents and purposes, everything he proposed came true including the removal of customs posts and, at least in design aspects, a 'single' passport, and they're even talking now about a single currency and it looks like it could happen. Interesting, isn't it? You know, IG Farben even suggested the same in answer to a request for a blueprint for a new 'economic order' in Europe from the Nazi government; common currency, common laws and a European Court. It all started with the 'European Coal and Steel Community'. Big industries shaping the future whilst making big money and the Germans still had big industries, many of them derived from IG Farben." He looked into his empty cup and wandered off to the kitchen leaving us to contemplate his words.

As the days passed, Fin visited his FBI contact, the former top hacker, and left all our new information with him. The guy was particularly pleased to know the real identity of 'The Innominate'. He'd claim that victory for himself but we were ok with it, we wanted a low profile. What we needed to do now was move on to Silverman, follow the trail. We didn't have any photographs of him but I remembered Emil said Lars had worked at Bełżec on construction, if Silverman 'drew up' the plans maybe Lars could ID him. I knew it was a long shot but it was all I had.

Speaking to Emil, I could see he was uncomfortable with the idea. "Emil, we can go down there, get some reconnaissance pictures and send them over to you for him to take a look at. If he recognises him, then we go to work," I'd said.

"I don't know, Eugene, he's put all of this into his past and I more than anyone knows how hard it is to open that door back up again. He had a life with his wife, Panni, who passed away some years back from tuberculosis. He has his cherished memories and I know they're important to him, I really do, but I just don't think it's fair to open him up to all of this," he'd said.

"I understand Emil, it's a big ask, don't you worry, we'll find another way." As I walked out of Emil's study, I bumped into Lars in the hall causing him to drop something on the floor. I picked it up for him.

"Thank you," he said then, "You look like you have the weight of the world on your shoulders, my friend, can I help?"

The temptation was strong but I had to honour my boss's wishes. "No, I'm fine, just trying to work things out a little," I replied.

I drove at speed to Fin's. "How many people got out of Bełżec? Someone must still be alive that can identify Silverman as possibly being The Architect." I told him.

"It didn't go well then I assume," Fin replied.

"No, but I have to be fair, Emil thought about it but eventually it was his friend he worried for, and I understand that. We have to find another survivor," I said. It wasn't going to be easy.

Later that evening, Emil phoned for an update, so we passed the news back to him, but then he already knew only a handful had survived Bełżec. He spoke of Lars, something that had come up in conversation, "He told me he knew of Hans Schröder and Otto Weiss.

Schröder was the name I thought I'd recognised, the name I couldn't quite place. It must have been in the files somewhere and just stuck in my memory. Lars told me he saw them at Bełżec, they stayed a couple of days. Anyway, he wants in on the operation, he wants to help us."

"How did a conversation like that start," I asked.

"I don't know, it just surfaced, he was asking how the work was progressing and what we were working on. I mentioned we had Rudi Baumann arrested and he said he too had spent some time at Bełżec, but I can't verify that within the Sikora files. Maybe you can look into Stahnke's files, you never know. Anyway, Lars wants to help us and that's the up and down of it all, it's of his own accord, I didn't encourage him. I just can't deny the man, he deserves to be a part of this," Emil said.

"Emil, that's great news, so can we ask Lars if he'll identify Silverman as The Architect?" I asked.

"Why do you think I'm calling you? I knew you'd be excited by the news, I saw the disappointment in your face the other day. You're a good boy, Eugene, you didn't once pester me any further on the matter, you showed great respect, that's why I'm calling, to let you know we're all going on a little trip to Chile.

Silverman lived on the outskirts of Mendoza. As a travelling group we'd stand out, so we booked the flights and hotels separately. Fin and I would stay in a place called Membrillo Inn, the older guys were booked into a place on the other side of town called 'Palacios'. Emil had said it looked pleasant enough, with decent facilities, but we hadn't booked in for a holiday, it was time to get down to work.

It seemed like a boys' adventure as we left Idar Court but we all knew how serious a situation we were entering into, anything could happen on this trip, we had to have our wits about us. If he was who we thought he was we knew we'd all be dead men if there was the slightest leak of information. Stahnke had told us Silverman knew who gave the 'Final Order' and if he knew that we figured he knew all about the plans the Nazi's made after the war.

Fin was uncomfortable on the flight, as usual. I questioned him about it and he told me there was good reason, apparently back in the day, he'd been on a light aircraft as a Navy Seal, the mission was to drop into enemy territory at low altitude to avoid radar. It was, he said, "The first-ever real base jump. People do it for fun nowadays. We set off at around two hundred feet and descended, each of us had been specifically trained for the operation, but it would be me that got caught out. It was a risk we took and accepted. Hell, it was the most frightening thing I've ever been through. I never liked heights at the best of times. I was just doing my job but it kind of made me dislike heights even more when it was over," he said.

"So how did it all end up," I asked him.

"I hit the trees hard, broke an ankle and damn near ripped my ass off. But we got the mission done," he said.

"Weren't you in pain?" I asked.

He looked at me as if I was kinda strange. "Oh, yeah, but I took some meds, got on and did my job," he explained.

We landed, exhausted, at El Plumerillo International Airport after a thirteen-hour long flight. Just a twenty-minute drive to our accommodation, we took two hire vehicles, splitting ourselves so as not to appear conspicuous, we took no chances. To come this far in such a short time and then to blow it all because of not planning properly wasn't an option. Emil and Lars headed off to 'Palacios,' and Fin and I headed to the Membrillo Inn. Turned out the Inn had seen better days. The room smelt damp and the linen looked well worn. I got a shower to try to make myself feel a little fresher, but drying off with a towel I wouldn't have used to clean a dog with, had the reverse effect. In the bar, I said to Fin, "I bet you those two guys are in the lap of luxury. I should have known with a name like 'Palacios' they'll both be sat sipping expensive brandies by now."

"Get the beer in and let's just run over our plans," Fin said without hesitation or disappointment in his tone. I guess he'd stayed places much worse.

We sat facing each other at a table by the window, running through what we were about to go do the following day.

"Remember, surveillance always comes first, we sit tight, we watch and we find out, we report back to Emil and take it from there," Fin said.

Emil told me the USA and Chile had a mutually agreed extradition treaty in place that we could call upon, if necessary, to bring Silverman back to America to face charges in relation to any war crimes that we discovered but our preference was not to use that, it was time-consuming and too public. Our main objective wasn't to capture 'The Architect,' it was to name the man who gave the 'Final Order.' We just needed Silverman to co-operate, to say the word, and maybe we'd find Otto Weiss or Hans Schröder.

I called Emil, he seemed pleased when he told me, "You know, Eugene, I have a feeling about this man, it's obvious to me he's worked very closely with Albert Speer, he had his patronage. We could, if we wanted, push ourselves down the road of proving Speer knew all about the Holocaust and was a wilful player in the murders, but he's dead and that would achieve nothing. I am tempted but I want it second only to finding out Schröder was the man who gave that gutless Final Order. We have to look at the bigger picture. What could we take out of the knowledge gained from such a finding? Would it lessen the impact of the denouncement of Hans Schröder as the man who, upon realising the war was lost, activated the order to kill the remaining Jews in the concentration camps of Europe?

Only a man with a heart full of hatred and spite would have given that Final Order, a man with a dark and sinister reason possibly to continue the fight."

I knew Emil had an obsession with Speer which he was trying to rein in but it was there, nevertheless. I wanted to reinforce his newfound focus so I told him, "I can see our goal clearly in my head, it's simple, as you told me right at the beginning, focus on our objective. Ours is to find the man who gave 'The Final Order,' it isn't to prove that Speer knew about the Holocaust or that Adolf Hitler somehow survived Berlin, you said not to go down blind alleyways, Emil, and my experience says that's just what we could be doing. Don't get me wrong, I totally understand why, but I think we are taking our eyes off the ball. We need to focus on the things we've achieved, we've come a long way in a short time, finding the Belsen Files in Ilse Gerver's loft, identifying Kasper Stahnke and realising he had much more information about the Nazis than *we* could possibly use, and now I feel we're at a turning point in the road. We either stay on it, play with what we believe about Hans Schröder, or we risk losing that to prove a dead man knew about the Holocaust and didn't feel the rope tighten around his neck."

"Of course I know your right, Eugene, living through my eyes, it's hard sometimes to keep it all real and do what Aleksy told me to do. I'm sure even he ventured down the wrong path sometimes, maybe the book you found was one of those paths," he said.

I'd forgotten all about the Speer biography. "Have you had the chance to read it yet," I asked.

"Yes, I wanted to talk to you about it, my copy is a little burnt around the edges but it still retained some markers I think Aleksy may have made, just a few paragraphs underlined, very interesting. I'll speak to you about it soon. It's been a long day and I need some sleep." he said.

I'd read about half the book in my spare time, to be honest, nothing jumped off the pages and made me look deeper so I was intrigued, but it could wait. Albert Speer was a very interesting man, but a very strange character. The only thing that struck me was he was intelligently superior to all other top Nazi's.

Once again, I dreamt that night, it was the winter of 1945, snow fell all around me, yet I sat in a park with a newspaper looking at the birds flying all around me. I read the news about the hanging of Irma Grese, a fellow guard of Ilse Gerver's. Her execution was administered with a judicial hand but somehow within my dream, the judge had passed sentence at the same time as Albert Pierrepoint pulled the lever that dropped her through the doors to her death, the rope quickly tightening around her throat and snapping her neck with violent force. In the dream, I wondered how Gerver would've been feeling, awaiting her own trial knowing of Grese's death.

I had a new life within my sleep at night. It puzzled me when I woke why I'd never had such vivid dreams before. Sure, I'd had dreams but not like these, so real, I could smell, feel, touch and taste within them, but then I'd been puzzled a lot by my slumber induced imaginings since I met Emil Janowitz and took on the role of his detective. I guess part of the learning to deal with the events we were dealing with is allowing your subconscious mind to catch up and learn along with you.

The surveillance was slow going, we took turns in taking watch on the property Silverman was supposedly at but we began having doubts after four days of virtually no movement. A woman went in on the Tuesday around midday, she didn't come out and the building was shuttered so we couldn't get a look in on anything. After the fifth day, Fin said, "We'll have to do something, we can't sit around getting nowhere, what are you like with heights, Gene?" Something like that, from him, naturally put me on my guard. "What do you have in mind Fin?" I asked.

"It's a long shot but I've got some miniature cameras we can drop down those chimneys, this time of year they won't be lighting any fires and we could take a look inside the property. You'll need to get on the roof from the back of the house, it's not overlooked," he said.

"Jesus, Fin, you've had this planned all along you son of a bitch, ok talk me through it," I replied.

We ran through my approach, I was going to come into the rear garden from the woods beyond. "There's only about twenty-five metres where you'll be out in the open so you'll need to move fast, then get tight to the building, use the garage to give you a boost up to the roof proper. See that small ladder?" he pointed as he spoke, "it has five rungs on it, just enough to perfectly get you onto the garage, then take it up with you and use it to get up to the next level, vice versa on the way down."

I crouched down in the woods behind the house, Fin at a distance with Lars, listening for updates on his radio. I used mine with an earpiece. The back of the house was shuttered up. I watched, checking any movement of the security cameras, noting their field of vision. I reckoned I'd be camera visible for about 10 seconds. I timed my run and emerged from the woods with the surveillance equipment in a small drawstring bag over my shoulder. The flexible videoscope inspection system we were using was a simple set-up that could be monitored from a distance of 200 metres.

I ran as quickly and quietly as I could across the lawn towards the rear of the house. I made it to a blank wall, to my right the garage with the small ladder leaning against it next to a small clear glass window through which I saw there was a connecting door to the house. I got to the roof in two manoeuvres, taking the ladder with me. Gently and quietly, I made my way up to the chimney stack, used the ladder to gain height and took the equipment out, lowering it carefully.

"A little more, go real slow Eugene, I can see light appearing below," Fin informed me. "There's an opening just below, about a foot further, go gently," he said. "Six inches now, we just need it slightly below, we don't want it visible. Gene. Ok stop, we're in. Get yourself back here."

I secured it in position and slowly made my way down the roof, noticing a few wasps and suddenly realised I'd somehow disturbed a nest in the rafters below. All of a sudden there was a swarm emerging and I knew I had to get down real quick. I left the ladder and just jumped to the garage roof, then down again to the garden, twisting my ankle a little as I hit the lawn but I was still able to make it back to the woods. I limped my way through the trees and got back to Fin.

"The woman's passed through the room several times," he said. "But we need a sighting of Silverman."

As we sat watching the monitor, a man entered the room, at first it wasn't clear how old he was but as he drew nearer to the fireplace we decided this was possibly our man. I turned to look for acknowledgement from Lars, he nodded, it was Silverman. "That's him, I even recognise his walk, the mole under the right eye, see there," he pointed at the monitor. "He's old like us all, but it's him, he's The Architect," he said. I looked at Emil's friend thinking to myself, '*He knew to call him The Architect.*' Maybe Emil had mentioned the term to him? I pondered for no longer than a few moments, "Are you definite Lars, we have to be sure," I asked, "Yes, definite," he replied.

I called Emil with the news. "What's the next move," I asked him. "Well, Eugene, here's the crux of the matter, we need him to tell us who gave the Final Order, but I think he can offer much more. I know Fin's brought some of his sodium thiopental with him and I'd be curious to see what that could offer us regarding answers from Silverman. The problem is, if we kidnap him he'd likely be missed, we know there's a woman inside the house and security cameras but it looks as though that is all, no guards, so I'm thinking we could go into the property, use the sodium thiopental on both of them, extract what we need and get out. He'd be none the wiser the next day. We don't know who the woman is, she may be an innocent maid as far as we know so we must approach this with caution," he said.

"Ok, I think that's all possible, it won't be easy but it can be done, I'll talk with Fin about a plan. I don't want to jeopardise the operation by taking Lars, Emil, he wouldn't be an asset to this," I told him.

"No, I appreciate that, Eugene, and I wouldn't expect you to do that, he'll be fine with me," he replied.

Fin and I sat up that night until the early hours, planning it out, ensuring everything was checked thoroughly. Once in, with the shutters seemingly permanently down, we could control the situation and be free to do what we needed without any prying eyes.

The following night, having housed them both in the property, we avoided the cameras, timing our run to the wall and gained entry via the garage and the connecting door I'd seen when grabbing the ladders. Fin was adept at lock picking, within seconds we were closing the door gently behind us and creeping through the house, night vision goggles on. We moved from room to room with stealth. Entering the bedroom, they both lay sleeping quietly, clearly partners. It made things easier. We administered chloroform at the same time, with virtually no resistance. Fin worked fast, managing to get Silverman up over his shoulder and moving him towards the living room we'd passed just before. I tied the woman up so she couldn't cause any interference if she came round and placed tape carefully over her mouth leaving her nasal passage free to breathe; we didn't want to suffocate her.

Suddenly, an alarm went off. I scrambled along the hall to where Fin stood in a doorway. "We can't leave him, we've got to take him with us, it's the only way," he shouted.

It wasn't how we'd planned it, in fact, it had gone disastrously wrong, but it was the only option left open to us; get 'The Architect' out and deal with the rest of it once he was secure.

Silverman still over Fin's shoulder, we left the way we entered and made through the woods towards the car we'd parked up earlier. Fin placed him in the rear seat, laying him down, out cold, but gave him a shot, a little sodium thiopental, to ensure he didn't wake whilst I rang Emil to give him the bad news.

"It hasn't gone quite to plan, he's in the back of the car with us now, we need a safe house ASAP," I said. "It's just as well I took precautions, Eugene, head over toward Palacios. I hired a garage to house the car, I thought it may be of use if things went awry, it's round the back about a hundred yards from the Hotel, I'll be in there waiting with the light on," he said.

Now, we had a big problem. The garage wasn't soundproofed and was one of several in a small industrial estate. With the car inside there wasn't room to swing a cat. Emil didn't appear phased by it all. He simply told us to sit tight, that he'd planned for this eventuality and he'd come back to us soon.

José Castillo was a fat-faced ageing pilot, who'd run flights for the Medellin Cartel headed by Pablo Escobar in the seventies, his association with Cuca Moreno, 'The Chemist', had brought him within the Cartel. He'd escaped prosecution by pure luck after Escobar's cartel folded in 1993 and had kept his Beech Queen AirB80 to run charters privately ever since.

I took a dislike to him from the start. He began renegotiating his fee. No sooner were we up in the air, he said, "I could turn around and hand you over to the authorities. $100,000, is the price for my silence." Fin slipped the knife from his pocket and held it against Castillo's cheek. "This is how I silence people."

"Can any of you fly this thing? I thought not," he replied, he was right of course, he had us at a disadvantage, and Emil knew it. "$100,000 is fine, I'll wire it through to your chosen account as soon as you get us onto American soil," he reluctantly replied.

The flight hadn't got off on the right foot, we'd struggled with Silverman. He was hooded and the drugs we were using, if used too regularly, were detrimental to his health at his age, so we used them sparingly, if and when necessary. When we explained the situation to him and the fact the woman hadn't been killed just put under sedation, he settled down a little.

"My wife, she won't understand any of this, I met her after the war," he'd said. We didn't care, at that stage, it was hit and miss whether any of us would make it through to American soil or not, the flight was horrendous and I could see Fin wasn't at his best, the turbulence was throwing us around quite violently, but Castillo told us everything was fine. I wasn't too sure and could tell Fin wasn't either.

Emil sat with Lars, both seemed at ease with the situation unfolding before us. "It's only a little turbulence, it will pass," Emil had said calmly, like a father to his children, but the turbulence was sporadic and continued for quite some time. It would be a long flight with refuellings and a stopover to ensure we hit Texas in the very early hours, Castillo using somewhere familiar, we assumed from his drug-running days. We all sat cramped up into a small fuselage, trying to wish the time away, but it got the better of Fin when Silverman started to come round, the drugs wearing off. Attempting to struggle out of the bindings that held his hands together, Fin slapped him around the head, I think the stress had gotten to him. Now an old man, it didn't go down well with Emil.

"Findlay," he shouted abruptly. "That's not the way we do things, we're better than the animals that imprisoned me, we will not strike Mr Silverman or show him violence, for all we know about the man at the moment, he may well have been a victim himself. We treat him correctly, Mr Quinn, and that's final."

Fin apologised and then said to Silverman, "Please don't try any further moves, you can't exactly go anywhere anyway."

"I think that's the point, you're tying me up when we are mid-air? I can understand once we land, but these bindings are hurting," Silverman replied. Emil nodded and Fin undid them. The hood, however, remained on.

When released, Silverman said, "Why have you done this? I'm nobody important, I live a quiet life alone with my wife."

"We believe you are the man known to us as 'The Architect' and that you have knowledge of the whereabouts of Hans Schröder, the person we suspect of giving the 'Final Order' to exterminate the Jews of Europe," Emil replied.

Who are you? Are you Mossad? This is all a big mistake. I'm Jewish myself and I'm not an architect, I'm an accountant but if that's all you want, turn the plane around, get me back to my wife, I can tell you all you need to know in five minutes. You didn't need to go to all this bother," he said.

Emil smiled. "Well, you see extraditing you wasn't an option, your kind of people throw money at situations, thinking you're above the law, thinking you can get away with your crimes, but not this one Mr Silverman, not this one."

Chapter 9

Joy Division

The landing wasn't much better than the flight, we hit the 'runway' so hard I thought the tyres would burst. We were on a tarmac road that led off from the TX-16. Fin had arranged it; an old pal had land out there with a couple of buildings we could use. Guided in by radio and the sparse placing of some tactical lighting, the pilot came to a dead stop and we were met by two black vans, with heavily tinted windows. With military precision, they had us in the back of one and away, the other followed on, the driver remaining with us in case we needed assistance. Castillo took straight off, disappearing into the night.

I'd just had the worst flight of my life and one I would never take again. I looked at Fin with some understanding at that moment, realising the fear he must have gone through.

"You ok?" I asked.

"I am now, just glad to get off that bucket of bolts," he replied.

We'd sprung Silverman on Emil with very little time to organise a thing, so it was to his great credit he'd not only arranged a flight out from Chile, but he'd also got us a pilot who had the experience of flying below radar, avoiding any international incident arising from the abduction. They would know he'd been taken, but by who would remain a mystery to them. The authorities would be looking for the usual suspects, drug cartels and other organised crime. Castillo certainly wouldn't spill the beans on us, he'd implicate himself and, importantly for us, make himself and the business he ran much too visible.

"How far are we going?" Silverman asked.

"We're taking you somewhere safe, and if you co-operate there's nothing to worry about," Emil replied

It was a fifteen-minute drive to the safe house and although not luxurious it had what was necessary. A separate outhouse served to provide washing and toilet facilities. I guessed it was used by the ranch hands from time to time.

As he sat Silverman down on a chair, holding onto his bound hands to steady him, Emil began the questions.

"I want you to explain to me your betrayal, so I can understand why you did what you did," he first asked.

"My name is Jonah Silverman, you're holding me against my will, I have no idea why you called me The Architect and I demand you let me go," he replied.

Emil hesitated as if searching inside for some calmness. "You can demand all you want, so now let's stop fooling around, you said you could give me the location of Hans Schröder, I'd like that information, but first of all, Mr Silverman, I want you to explain to me why you assisted Albert Speer in the construction of the gas chambers at Auschwitz and Bełżec camps?"

Silverman sighed. "I assisted in the camps because I had no choice but I had nothing to do with construction, I only dealt with the money, they had my family and used my sister within what they called laughingly 'the Joy Division'. She was raped by Nazi soldiers every night until the light of life left her eyes and she killed herself, unable to bear what they were doing to her any longer," he explained.

"I understand your pain, it is such a terrible thing but you haven't really answered my question, you see, my mother and little sister Anna were taken to the gas chambers you helped create, my brother Filip and my father died inside the camp you assisted in building with Albert Speer, so I ask you why did you betray your people? We all suffered, the children suffered, I just want you to be honest and tell me exactly why you chose to assist and collaborate with the Nazi's and especially Speer in their master plan."

Both Fin and I kept quiet, Emil hadn't told us he was going down this route, it was clearly personal and he'd not let go of his obsession with Speer.

"Mr Silverman, I will ask you again to tell me and only me. This isn't an interview, I'm just an old Jew asking why you aided the Nazi's to kill my family, I just need to know your reason," Emil said.

"My reason was nothing to do with your family," Silverman responded. "I had to find a way to survive just like everybody and I told you I had nothing to do with construction, I was one of the lucky ones who could offer a skill, I had a use to them. I was and still am an accountant."

Emil wasn't giving up. "No, I'm sorry that's not a reason or the answer I want to hear. I had skills and many others had them, but we didn't collude to make it easy for the Nazi's to kill our own kind. You see, Mr Silverman, I see you as a traitor, a Judas that colluded to help kill my family."

Jonah Silverman had had enough. Firmly, he replied, "Well, what can I say? I tried to look after my own family, nothing I say will placate you so ask your questions and do what you wish with me. I can tell you lots of things. Do you want the location of the carpet Adolf Hitler was allegedly rolled up in before they burned his body? I can give you that and it will disprove all the history books, you won't find Hitler's blood stains on that roll of carpet. You want the Russian diagnosis of the skull fragments taken from the bunker that prove it's a woman's skull, not the Führer's?" He paused. "You see, there are many conspiracies of what happened after the war, the interesting thing is none of them have any evidential proof, don't you find that extremely strange?"

I interrupted. "So you're telling me you can prove Hitler lived after Berlin fell?"

"No, I didn't say that did I? But, one gun shot was heard within the bunker at the time of Hitler's suicide pact with his wife, the skull has the entry point of that shot and the Russians say it was a woman's, probably Eva Braun, so that leaves a mystery doesn't it? And, if I told you Albert Speer left the bunker and flew out of Germany which some say is heavily documented, would it surprise you if there was a possibility Hitler went along with him and boarded the submarine U-530 and escaped to Argentina, would that surprise you?" he asked me.

"Well. it all sounds like a pile of possibles and maybes to me, although you probably know they found Hitler's jaw bone with some of his teeth attached and they were identified from his dental records so if he made it to Argentina he did it without his mouth." Fin sniggered, "Probably why we haven't heard from him for such a long time."

I hadn't finished. "Enough of the bullshit and let's get on with the facts, Jonah," I said. "There is no Hitler carpet, they burnt it after they burned the bodies, Speer didn't fly out of Germany, he may have flown out of Berlin but he only got as far as Flensburg which is where they arrested him. You're smoke and mirrors, Jonah. It's almost as if you were following a set script."

I stopped the others from cutting in, something had just occurred to me. "Who do you work for, Mr Silverman? You said you're still an accountant. Who are your clients?"

"I have several private clients," was all he said but I saw his body tense up.

"You work for Forge Ore, don't you," I told him.

"I have private clients and they will remain that way."

"When was the last time you saw Hans Schröder? You know where he is," I said with certainty in my voice. "You've worked for him recently, I'd bet, and Otto Weiss."

Emil stepped forward. "Tell me about Speer. You worked closely with him, he must have confided in you?"

Silverman's head bowed, he sounded exhausted. "I don't know anything about Speer. I never met the man. I didn't design any camps or anything in them. Yes, I was their accountant, I have told you that. First, I was in Auschwitz. It was Dejaco who was in charge of designing the chambers and crematoria there. In

November '41 they sent me to Bełżec to be the accountant on its construction. Thomalla was responsible for its building and operation. I must have impressed him, he asked me to do some work for him, personal work. Then others there wanted my services. They were siphoning off the proceeds of the killings. They promised they would look after my family who I'd had to leave in Auschwitz. Then Thomalla took me with him when he went on to construct Sobibor and Treblinka. I didn't live with the main population, they housed me with the Trawniki guards. I was at Treblinka when Schröder arrived there to speed things up. On the recommendation of Thomalla, Schröder asked me to do some work for him. He actually *asked* me but I knew I couldn't refuse. When it was obvious that Treblinka was finished as a 'reception center' I thought it would be the end for me, I knew what they did to the 'sonderkommando' in these places but Schröder had me transferred back to Auschwitz. Not to Birkenau, you understand. My family were in Birkenau. I never saw them again. After the war, I discovered mama and papa had been sent to the gas chambers not long after I'd left. My wife, her cousin and my brother the SS had kept alive but they were placed on the death march to Belsen. My brother died during this, someone told me they shot him for arguing with a guard over their treatment of the women. The two girls, I was told, died from typhus not long after arrival." He took a deep breath and began sobbing. "You think I contributed to the deaths of all those people? Do you think I was a willing accomplice? I did what I had to do to keep my family alive for as long as I could."

Fin cut in."Why does your name appear on a list of construction workers?"

Silverman didn't hesitate. "Because I was the accountant for those works. There'll be one or two other names on there, they'll be the overseer and the SS guard in charge of that detail. The rest will simply be numbers. I never made the lists and I didn't take part in the constructions. I simply costed the works for the SS Hauptamt."

I looked at Fin, he nodded slowly back to me with a slight shrug of his shoulders.

I decided to ask the obvious question but there was compassion in my voice now, "Jonah, why are you still working for Schröder?"

"He contacted me, after the war. I don't know how he found me, he's never said. He told me he did all he could to save my family but his instructions were never carried out or simply ignored. I believed him and I think I still do because he wasn't there at the end, he'd returned to Berlin."

"And you're their accountant."

He nodded his head.

Fin took me aside, "I think we should let him rest now, help me get him to the bed." Emil sat by a table, he looked stunned. Lars sat where he'd sat all along, in an easy chair against the far wall, still saying nothing.

As we guided him to his feet, Jonah Silverman said, "If you've done your research, you know Dejaco and Thomalla are long dead. I have told you the truth, but you want Hans Schröder, you want the man who you believe gave the 'Final Order', the one that said to kill the remaining Jews of Europe?"

Emil replied, "Yes, it's important to all survivors, for the people who lost their families so unnecessarily."

We helped Silverman to the wooden cot in the corner and as we lay him down, he said, "Nobody but you has ever thought him important enough to hunt down. Look for Dietmar Wolff. He changed his name and became a respected member of society in La Cumbrecita. He's an Argentine citizen now."

Emil wanted to ask another question but Fin stopped him, "Emil, the guys whacked, What with the drugs, the flight and the general shock, I'm worried if he doesn't get some rest and we push him too hard he's gonna have a heart attack."

We removed the hood, replacing it with a sleep mask as a blindfold and then we let him sleep.

We unloaded some light provisions from the van outside, then the driver, who introduced himself as 'Marty' handed us the keys so we could go somewhere to get a signal on the mobiles. We had to drive for an hour before we were successful and Fin called a guy he knew. "Hi, Frog. I need to speak to the Bear, it's urgent." There was a pause, probably only fifteen seconds but it seemed longer. "Bear, I need a favour. You still test driving that new software for Homicide? If I give you some details can you slip this one in? I'm trying to find a guy in Argentina."

While we waited I asked Fin what was so special about the software his friend was testing. "Well, Gene, normally you have to laboriously do the individual searches. This thing is a homicide investigation tool and one of the things it does is to cross-reference the whole internet, bank records, birth and death records, marriage and criminal records. It's pretty neat."

After a couple of hours spent at the side of a lonely road, we had all we felt necessary to move forward.

Marty had taken first watch allowing the 'old folk' to get some sleep and when we got back he rustled up some chow for us all then got his head down.

We sat, after the meal, discussing the current situation. Emil, I could tell, still wanted Speer to be involved in all this so we called a vote. Lars declined, saying he was, strictly speaking, only along as a witness and observer. Fin and I voted Emil down. The thing was we both felt we'd started to lose sight of what the facts were telling us. We'd almost come to believe that 'The Architect' *and* the perpetrator of the final order was the same person. The evidence, as we knew it now, was telling us that Schröder was 'the architect' of the 'Final Order' but 'The Architect' of Stahnke's betrayal story, the architect of the Auschwitz and Bełżec gas chambers was someone else entirely.

Silverman woken and fed, the interrogation began again:

"What records did you keep working for Forge?"

"In the old days it was all paper, Hans and Otto kept the bulk of things but I have some in boxes in my basement. I haven't looked at them in years, I've no idea what's there."

"How are they kept now?"

"It's all on the computer?"

"Yours?"

"Do you think they are stupid? Their computer system."

"But you know the entry codes?"

"Of course I do."

"How do you know Kaspar Stahnke?"

"I don't know anyone of that name."

We kept at it for an hour. He didn't change his story one bit. We took a break outside, got some sunshine.

Fin broached the subject first. "Emil, we have to hand this guy over to the FBI. He'll be far more useful to them than to us now."

I agreed but Emil thought he knew more about Speer than he was telling.

Fin disagreed. "I think he's telling the truth, Emil. We've got what we needed from him. Our target was Schröder and we have what we wanted. We have to move on. The whole Forge and Fourth Reich thing is beyond our capabilities. Only the Feds can handle that now."

He was right but how were we going to get around the abduction issue? He had it covered. "We tell him the truth. He can't go back now. When they find out he's missing, and they will, they'll assume the worst. He's a walking dead man. We owe him something. I'm sure he'll be willing. We tell the FBI he wants to co-operate and surrendered himself to us. I figure they won't want to ask us too many searching questions. We'll use your friend, Collins, as the conduit, Emil."

When Silverman realised what we were telling him was his only practical option all he said was, "You have to get my wife out there, please, I'll do whatever's wanted of me but get her away from them."

"Jesus H Christ, Emil, you just can't do these kind of things, you'll cause an international incident you crazy son of a bitch," Cooper Collins was clearly heard saying over the mobile as Emil called in with his update.

"It needed doing and it's done, we have to deal with it now Cooper, he's already given me Schröder, he'll give the FBI much more, I promise you that," Emil replied. "This man is a target for every ardent Nazi in the world now, we'd be hanging him out to dry if we simply return him.

"Emil, you should have told me your plans."

"You'd have tried to stop us, Coop."

"You're damn right! I don't know if I can help you and I'm not promising anything but I'll try, you crazy old bastard. This is my job on the line here."

Emil just replied, "Don't worry about your job, you can come work for me, I pay much better and we can sort out a pension plan. But I have another favour to ask. I take it Stahnke is in the county jail. Eugene needs to speak to him again, can you get him access?"

"Ok, Emil, leave it with me, I'll see what I can do but for the love of Jesus don't you do one single thing more," he ended the conversation.

"I don't think he's pleased with us, boys," Emil said whilst raising an eye.

We had to move fast. Fin decided he'd do the job himself, it'd take too long for him to put a team together. He left that afternoon for a commercial flight to Chile, he'd check the place out, hire muscle if needed, speak to the local FBI agent telling them about the availability of the free evidence in the basement for a matter already under investigation and leave it with them. His main concern was Silverman's wife and he was hoping he'd get there quick enough to simply walk out the front door with her and get to the airport.

I asked him if he'd be ok with the flight. He smiled and replied, "Hell, after that last one this'll be like a holiday."

In the meantime, Emil found us somewhere else to live. San Antonio. It was perfect, a big place and we wouldn't stand out there like we would in the towns closer to our original stop. Fully paid up on a month lease, it had all we needed including internet access. The restrictions were off for Silverman and we weren't hiding our identities anymore. We told him he was free to leave but he'd be on his own and he knew it. He also knew we'd have his wife soon.

The information Fin got with his homicide software enquiry led us to research on La Cumbrecita. It was a place within Argentina that earned its name 'Little

Germany,' the street signs were in German, the restaurants serve schnitzel and gulasch while the delis and bars sold jars of homemade sauerkraut and Bavarian beer. It seemed the escaping Nazi's had made a home from home within the borders of their haven in Argentina. We concentrated on the name Silverman had told us, Dietmar Wolff, finding the name change had occurred back in 1973, that was the coincidence we'd been looking for. Just before FORGE ore was founded, Schröder had disappeared and now we knew why. He'd left his fellow Nazi's in charge of what looked like his own project, Otto Weiss had taken over at the exact time Schröder had changed his name to Wolff and because of Fin's information we'd been able to pinpoint exactly the time, date and registry office his name change had taken place at. La Perla was the nearest town of note and it held the record of Hans Schröder's name change. From there our next record found was 1979 when, seemingly feeling comfortable, he put himself forward in a local election for town mayor. I'd found the nomination records, but he withdrew shortly after, but it left a trail though, so he was still around in '79. From that, I got an address and the land registry files showed there was no change of ownership since that date so he was either still living there or, at least, still owned it.

A few days later Fin phoned with an update, "I've got her, no problems encountered and we're on our way back," was all he said.

I kept digging through the internet and found a picture of Wolff from a local Argentine newspaper. He'd attended a big money function and was named on the photo.

Then we got a call from Cooper Collins, it'd been a week since Emil had sown the seeds of what we wanted to do with Silverman.

"It's taken a lot of favours and Jesus, Emil, my ass is on the line with this, I've got him into their witness protection programme and I'm gonna take you up on that job offer if it all goes belly up, but until then you owe me one, you owe me a big one, Emil. Take your guest to the San Antonio field office and tell them to contact Senior Special Agent Martinez in Albany."

As soon as Emil relayed this to me I told him we had to pack up and drop Silverman off at the field office before they organised themselves, possibly traced the mobile's signal and paid us a visit hoping to get a 'two for one deal'. Although I trusted the Feds, I didn't trust them so much that I'd risk being around to spend time in jail for kidnapping.

We explained to our 'captive' and told him that if he went in and handed himself over he'd be reunited with his wife within days, at the most. We also gave him a piece of paper with the FBI agent's name and office on it.

Taking a cab, we watched him walk in and when they took him away we headed for the airport.

When we got back to Idar Court, Fin was already there and Luiza was fussing over Silverman's wife. She stayed overnight and then we took her to the Albany FBI office where I explained I was simply security hired to ensure she got there safely, her husband being in the witness protection programme. They phoned Martinez and told *me* to take a seat. Whilst the receptionist was distracted I simply walked out. Fin was waiting to take me to my appointment with Stahnke at the Washington County jail.

I spoke with Emil, privately, some days later, he was having strange dreams again. He told me, "I was walking out of Auschwitz, a liberated man, there was nobody to stop me leaving and then I see the local people, all staring at me as I walked out of the gate. I saw Lars walking towards me, the people he was walking past weren't Polish, they were German, I could tell by their clothing and then I woke up. It felt like one of those dreams trying to tell you something. I don't know, but the local German civilians knew what was happening in the death factories, they were not as ignorant of the atrocities as they pretended. Even the Poles knew. The children would taunt the trains passing by, knowing where they were headed, and if the children knew then the population knew." He paused then said, "Strangely it's Lars who's been featuring within my dreams of late, he will play a part or role somewhere amongst the chaos of existence in Auschwitz, an observer of the many horrors I see within my dreams, all of which are genuine in terms they did happen, but Lars was not within my camp which puzzles me. Lars was in Bełżec. Maybe it's just confusion, the brain takes in so much information that it jumbles things around. Oh and the little bird, he is always there, sitting on the edge of the camp overlooking the site, it seems when all is lost and the people are being led to their deaths he sits watching, never moving from his fence, waiting for their spirits to be freed, a guardian of souls I think, ready to take them on to the next life."

I answered him quietly, "Maybe it's your minds way of coping, Emil, you've been through a hell of a lot lately, it will have stirred up memories of your past, I think that's inevitable. You couldn't have the memories you have and go through all we have in the last six months and not have it affect you in some way."

"Yes, you're right Eugene. I do find it helpful being able to talk to you, it gets things out of the system. I've never been able to do that, I never wanted to go through any form of therapy, I would find that clinical and cold, that's not how I should heal myself, I think I've done pretty well on my own, considering," he said.

I backed him up on that. "You've done fantastic Emil, I've only known you for a short time but I can see within you a strength of character. I want you to know I'm very proud to work for you and I think you're a good man," I said.

"You're a good boy, Filip," and he patted me on my shoulder, walking away totally oblivious to his Freudian slip and as always I let it pass, not wanting to upset him. I also didn't tell him what I and Stahnke spoke of.

The following day brought rain clouds, the sky was dark, filled with the storm it was about to unleash upon us, angry clouds formed above the apartment and at sea the weather would be wreaking havoc amongst the fishermen out trying to earn their living. I was pleased I wasn't one of them. I should have known it was a portent.

In the afternoon, I got a call. It was Emil. "Stahnke's dead."

"What the hell, happened?"

"Some neo-Nazi's got to him in the exercise yard. They were so many Cooper reckons it'll be difficult to pin down who actually did it. They slit his throat and his belly."

I was stunned. I'd only spoken to him a couple of days before. He'd told me what I wanted to know but had said, "Bruno, you got to get me out of here. What you did to me was a shit trick, getting me drunk and loosing my mouth off. I know I shouldn't have played games with you but this place is full of Nazis. You got to get me into the isolation wing. The longer I'm left out here in the general population, the more chance they'll get the word out and I'm dead meat."

I told him I'd do my best, but to be honest, I thought he was exaggerating. Nevertheless, I put a call into Cooper Collins, the following day. Now, I called him again and asked what had gone wrong. All he could say was, "I called the County Jail the same day, Gene, and sent over the paperwork right away but they say they never got it. Hell, I even sent the FBI a copy."

I knew it wasn't to keep his mouth shut, the Feds had the contents of his computer and floppys and I didn't think he had anything more to give. It was simply punishment for their loss.

When the weather cleared, with Fin and a small team back in South America, we took advantage of one of our 'in the bag' days. Jody and I drove out to Long Island, the Connetquot River State Park was somewhere we'd spent a little time before, it was an easy place to relax in, one you could take your mind off things, although my mind was struggling to do that. The job had gotten under my skin and into my bones, my hair had just started growing back after the undercover operation to ensnare Kaspar Stahnke, the scar on my arm hadn't yet healed properly and Jody hadn't forgiven me yet for doing such a 'damn fool thing,' I could still hear her voice telling me so.

"Nothing is more important than your health, Gene, Nothing," she'd angrily told me, then ran through several problems I could encounter, deliberately trying to worry me.

"Lyell's syndrome, erythema multiforme, necrotizing fasciitis and subacute cutaneous lupus erythematosus," were just a few of the things she told me could be heading my way if I didn't buck my ideas up.

None of it made any impact on me, I'd done it for a reason, a good one I thought, but I had to allow her to be upset and take it out on me because, in fairness, I'd have said much the same thing to her but maybe not so clinically.

Chapter 10

The Idea

Rested after the short break, Jody and I spent the whole weekend doing absolutely nothing, a walk in the woods was the sum total of our exertions, but it was a stunning place, the light at the time of the year seemed to shimmer off the leaves, it was the end of summer and the trees had just started fading to that wonderful shade that autumn offers, where everything was dying off but also at its most vibrant For a few weeks it would be just magical until fall set in and daylight surrendered too soon to the night sky.

I rang Emil to find he'd told Fin to come back. The enquiries down there had shown that Schröder still owned the property we'd traced but hadn't lived there himself for quite a few years. The people renting it paid to a real estate company which, no surprise, was a front of Forge's.

I wished I'd stayed a few more days with Jody in Long Island but still I helped Fin with some research, hoping to find something on the Schröder/Wolff enquiry, any little thing was a bonus we thought. But, for the first time, we were stumped, so Emil told us to utilise our time back on Hertha Bothe, which is where it all kind of started until we decided Ilse Gerver was an easier prospect. He hadn't given up on Bothe just yet, it still played on his mind, but as Fin told me, she'd covered her tracks well, serving her sentence and living a normal, everyday, life afterwards. He said her life after the war had been at the extremes of normality. Evading all questioning of her role, she'd served her sentence and expected to live her life out as a free woman. From what Fin told me, that was exactly how it had panned out up to now, at no point had she ever given any signs of talking or showing her side of the story, she'd taken out court orders to protect herself from enquiries and she'd wrapped herself in a cotton ball, living her life in hibernation. Fin was frustrated trying to even get a birth certificate from a local registry office, so well had she covered herself. I thought we'd be wasting valuable time on her, I told Emil that who asked me straight out, "What else are you going to fill your time with," and it was that moment I recalled the book I had been meaning to read, I'd put to one side because of my schedule and workload.

"I'd like to read the book about Speer, you know the autobiography I dropped at your house some months back," I said, Emil went into the living room and retrieved it, "Here, I've read it, there's nothing in it that will assist us, trust me, I scoured every damn page," he said whilst passing it over to me.

"Do you mind me reading it though, Emil? I think I'd prefer to stay on the ball with the case we're dealing with, I don't want to confuse the situation," I asked.

"Go ahead it's fine, a younger man's eyes may pick something up," he replied.

I spent several hours reading page after page, Speer's life unfolding before me, the book was well written, you got a feel of who the man was, a mix of two characters, high intelligence with incredible personality and the nervous shy man inside, he was a contradiction in terms.

Later that night after a nice meal with Jody and a walk round Madison Square Park, I sat in the window with a coffee bought earlier from *Grumpy's,* I'd picked my copy of the Speer book up and intended to spend half an hour on it, I was tired though and as I struggled to finish each page, I noticed my tiredness was making me not really take the contents in so I decided to get to bed, it had been a long day and I was sure I'd miss something important if I attempted to continue reading. I leant over to grab my bookmark off the table and as I did the book slipped from my lap onto the floor, falling open face downward, as I picked it up it was open on a page with a marking on, underlined pencil marks, in the margin, 'LK'.

I pondered for a moment what it could mean or represent but tiredness had taken a hold of me and I decided to address it the next morning, my brain just couldn't concentrate. I slept well that night, waking after another dream, this one was strange and I assumed my weariness had brought it about. I found myself in Emil's arms looking up at him, I felt terrible, weaker than I'd felt before, I looked up at him as he stroked my forehead, "It will all be alright, Filip, we will get out of here, I promise you," he said. Lars was there, for some strange reason, stood in the doorway opposite, my mind must have been jumbling life with fantasy. I floated above looking down on Emil then was back within the body Emil held in his arms. I felt the sensation of drifting in and out of consciousness, seeing bright white light but still feeling my *brother's* hands caressing my face, everything seemed calm and tranquil, all my aches and pains had disappeared, I felt nothing but peace. Then, everyone was below me, I was floating above my brother and the person laying in his arms, I was now overseeing the event instead of being part of it. Lars remained in the doorway. Just then an SS officer walked in, "I know what you did," he said and patted my brother on the back, Lars stood out of his way as he left the room and the door slammed shut.

I awoke confused as Jody stood over me with a cup of tea and a bagel, "Here sleepy head, you've got to go see Emil this morning. Did you stay up late,?" she asked.

"Er, no, I came up shortly after you, I was dog tired," I replied. "I had a weird dream, I dreamt Emil was my brother," I said out loud, not realising I was going to.

"Ahhh, did my baby have a little nightmare?" Jody teased.

I grabbed hold of her and pulled her onto the bed, "I'll give you a nightmare, you cheeky monkey," I said tickling her.

Picking up Speer's book again, I looked at the cover, he was just an ordinary-looking man, nothing exceptional, but he and his kind had caused the worst crime in mankind's long history. He wasn't a serial killer, nor a psychopath, although Hitler may well have been, Speer was just a day to day average man, ambitious and amenable. I wondered at what point he'd actually realised war crimes were taking place, what he had thought and why he hadn't done anything about it, not even a surreptitious diplomatic contact at a soirée. The book explained a lot to me, he spoke of things, but Emil had told me much more about the man than Speer's words could ever be honest enough to, I made my own opinion.

I also wondered what would happen to Silverman when it eventually came out that he was actually the man who, as Forge's accountant, had held the purse strings of the Third Reich after the war. Despite what he'd told us, the reality was that he'd benefited from the misfortune of others, for fifty years he'd lived unchallenged with a life of reasonable luxury, paid for from the blood of the victims of the Holocaust. I thought it was a job for others to think about, I'd done my part. My issue now was my realisation that something wasn't adding up and someone possibly wasn't all we thought they were. I needed to be cautious, revealing what I'd found out, too soon, could backfire on me.

I concentrated my thoughts on what was to be and how we'd execute our plan together. It would be like nothing we'd done before, we had to utilise everything we could. The Wiesenthal Centre, internal and international Law enforcement but there was only one problem, we couldn't trust any of them, we'd have to do all our planning in secrecy, using outsiders only when absolutely necessary. The Nazi's had power, and they had people in high places that could stop us in our tracks, worse still was the chance of Hans Schröder being tipped off, he'd go on the run and into hiding and we'd never find him. We'd have to work fast and do so with as small a unit of people as we could get away with. Cooper Collins would be first on the list, he knew people we *could* trust.

Chapter 11
The Plan

For days, nothing much happened. Fin had left a small team working Brazil and I'd asked Collins, on the spur of the moment, to see if he could get Silverman's phone records. When he got back to me we went through the list of incoming and outgoing calls with a fine-toothed comb. Only one thing stood out as odd. Every 6 weeks, he got a call from a public phone that would last around 30 to 40 minutes. The phone was listed for the town of Ponte Serrada, Brazil. A check of the calendar revealed he was due another call fairly soon.

Then we got another break. Fin's team came back with the information that they'd been supplied two addresses for Otto Weiss from the friend of a friend of a contact, someone who'd met the man and could point him out. The following days dragged by as we waited for an update.

When it came, it was better than we expected. Surveillance on both houses had led them to a bar where their informant had surreptitiously identified Weiss to them. The following day, Weiss and a younger companion, thought to be his protection, took a long journey that ended at a secure compound in a complex off the Chapecó River, in an area known as Baía Alta. No, they hadn't been able to confirm who lived there and tentative enquiries with a street cleaner revealed the place was popular with the Germans. The compound had security but it was pretty low key, a uniformed guard on the gate and a dog patrol together with a suit who the team reckoned might be 'carrying'. The name of the place seemed familiar.

A couple of well-placed phone calls later, I'd discovered the nearest town, only a few miles away, was Ponte Serrada. It was too much of a coincidence. That afternoon was spent making plans.

Over the next week, Emil and Fin recruited additions to our team. Coop was on board, with the confidence of falling back on Emil's offer, one way or another the guy had begun to enjoy flying by the seat of his pants whether it cost him his job or not and he was offering all the assistance in the aftermath he could.

The team would be seven in total, inclusive of myself, Fin, Lars, and Emil. It wasn't exactly what Fin and I had envisaged but Emil insisted and we needed Lars to hopefully identify Schröder. The rest of the crew consisted of a snappy dresser who Coop said was the best he'd seen in a long, long time, name of Gennaro Pirlo. He had that swagger about him and just didn't look like a cop, more a mobster. He reminded me of Vincent Corleone, actor Andy Garcia's character in the film 'The Godfather', but he came highly recommended. Another recruit was one of Fin's old colleagues Sean O'Mulligan, another Irishman who my colleague had worked with in the Bronx and the SEAL teams. Finally, there was Emilio Carballar, a former Army Ranger and a Mexican by birth but naturalised soon after, his parents had applied for their citizenship when Emilio was just a few months old and he'd been brought up in a little place off Pelham Parkway which I knew only too well. I'd arrested many people in the park there for dealing drugs but I'd also arrested a child killer in that very same place. Ivo Fletcher had murdered Ruby-Leigh Cameron, just a seven-year-old little girl who'd been entrusted into his care. I'd received a call on my radio to ID a perp within the park, he'd been reported by a parent for hanging around a playground, it was one of those moments you wished you'd paid more attention to the Crime Information sheets but hadn't. I arrested him on suspicion of loitering with intent but luckily a colleague had read the CI sheets and I was made aware that a detective in Greenwich PD was looking for Fletcher for the merciless killing of little Ruby-Leigh, a young innocent child.

I idly mentioned to Emil about the coincidence, Carballar living off the parkway, telling him about the Ivo Fletcher case I'd been involved in way back. "I had a very small role in capturing that guy," I'd told him.

"I know," Emil had replied whilst pausing for a moment. "I was the detective that took the case to court, I dealt with the family and saw the devastation that child's death had caused her parents. I still recall her father, that poor man suffered badly with guilt and he later hung himself, blaming the death of his only child on himself." I was shocked. I'd only had a minor role, I filled in my reports and handed them in, I really hadn't paid much attention to the roll-out of the case against Fletcher. Yeah, I gave testimony in court but then just left to go about my duties. I read a year or so later he'd gone to the 'chair' for his crime. I recall the New York

Times said how the execution hadn't gone quite to plan and it had taken him a while to die.

"You were the Greenwich PD detective?" I said. "Now that's some coincidence, Emil. We worked on the same case nearly fifteen years ago, you never told me."

"Eugene, I knew who you were when you first came for the interview. I had a head start on your background, you're a good cop and a good man, I knew you'd done your duty that day and knew I could trust you to do just that in our investigations," he said.

"Why did you not say anything, Emil?" I asked

"What point would that have served? Would you have walked away from the job, or maybe wanted it more, the point being I could trust you, you'd proven that before you even came for the interview, at that point in time, I needed you more than you needed the job. I needed somebody to trust with the files, the most important thing is I was right to trust you," he smiled.

I got the three new guys up to speed with the case and Fin took care of the military side of the operation, we'd had the Brazil team hire a light aircraft to do a general sweep over the area and now had some fairly detailed aerial pictures of Schröder's compound. I questioned the security he had on the place, I'd been expecting more but Fin told me, "The guys on the ground say the entire complex seems heavily German and they all seem to have a similar set-up. I'm thinking they're using a mutual aid system. If we get in there quick and neutralise his detail before an alarm can be sounded, it should be fine. If it goes wrong, I suspect you'll see plenty of security." I prayed for a successful extraction but took nothing for granted and asked we go over things again.

Meanwhile, my partner had sourced some transport, a UH-1 Iroquois twin-engined helicopter. Because the original single-engined version had once been designated the HU-1, all of this type became known as a 'Huey'. It came with a trusted pilot who'd flown for the CIA's 'Air America' in Vietnam-Laos in his younger days. Forests and jungles were no problem for this man, Fin assured me.

We got the confirmation from Brazil, they'd seen an old guy driven out then returned an hour later. He'd been for a haircut and a manicure in Ponte Serrada. One of the team had joined the queue in the barber's and heard the greeting, "Senhor Wolff, por favor, sente-se. Que bom vê-lo novamente."

We couldn't linger, we didn't have the luxury of time, so Fin and O'Mulligan headed off for a rendezvous in Paraguay where they'd also source some weapons whilst the rest of us flew to Sao Paolo and on to the nearest local airport to our target. To avoid suspicion, we stayed in a couple of hotels and a guesthouse in Chapeco, an hour and a half's drive away and arranged local vehicle hire through the hotels. We were paid up for a week stay but waited for Fin's confirmation within 24 hours.

He called early, they were ready, he gave me the coordinates of the rendezvous, a clearing in the forest over five miles up into the hills. We'd meet, kit up and, with the surveillance watching our asses, put the plan into operation, the last part of which was a low-level flight to Paraguay, briefly crossing Argentinian air space.

Chapter 12

The Night of the Long Knives

It was just as well we'd hired the 4 x 4s. We found the clearing at the end of a muddy mountain track and, shortly after, the distinctive sound of the Huey was upon us as it came in low over the trees, circled and put down. As the others collected kit bags and weapons Fin introduced me to the pilot, "This is Brick Dempsey, we go back a long way, Geno." We shook hands and I had to ask, "Is that your nickname or your real name?" I couldn't see the smile in the growing darkness as he replied, "It's a nickname, had to make one or two hard landings once upon a time. My real name's Clarence so you see why I'm happy with Brick."

The equipment was off, the engine noise increased and the Huey rose into the air then disappeared back over the trees and dipped down into the valley we couldn't see, taking the noise of the engine and rotors with it. Fin seemed to sense my thoughts, "It'll take him no more than ten minutes to get back here when we call him in."

With the exception of Emil and Lars, we loaded up. I had a pistol in a concealed holster and three magazines of 15 rounds each. The others, the ones with the training, sported the suppressed MP5K, a cut-down, real short sub-machine gun produced, ironically, by the Germans. With six 15 round magazines, the consensus was if that wasn't enough to accomplish something this night it was time to run away.

The plan was pretty simple. Wait for Wolff to go to bed then wait some more until we saw the signs of relaxation in the night shift security. The idea was to disable whatever resistance we met and shoot only as an absolute last resort. The surveillance updated us. They'd only seen one dog patrol at night, it patrolled the outside then went in for 30 minutes then patrol again. Their view into the compound wasn't good but tonight they'd seen two suits. Fin released them and told them to clear the area.

"I thought they were going to watch our asses?"

"That was my first thought but they're not armed and if we stir up a hornet's nest I don't want them getting caught up in it, they're going to come off worst," he replied.

It was time, the gate security guy brought a thermos flask and a thin chair out from his little sentry box and settled down. The dog man took his dog for another walk around the block. The animal out of the way made things a bit easier. In a side street, Sean, Emilio and Gennaro scaled the wall, night-vision goggles on and working. Fin and I pretended to have imbibed a bit too much as we approached the front gates.

At this point it was going well, the gate security officer interacted in a friendly manner and, as we hoped, allowed the two amiable drunks to get too close. Whilst I distracted him, Fin leapt on him with the chloroform soaked rag. We propped him in the chair against the sentry box, took his keys and opened the gate which led us into a small inner yard with a lit office in the corner. A quick check found it clear, the items that lay on the table told us it was where the dog man had been spending his time. Fin tried a few keys and the door into the main enclosure swung open. We were met by the sound of a dog suddenly barking, a cry of pain, silence quickly followed by the instant glare of floodlights and then gunshots. At the far end of the inner enclosure, the free-roaming guard dog had latched onto one of our colleagues with a vengeance and had to be shot but the game was up. As soon as the place was lit up the nightvison was useless and a hindrance. Ditching the kit, they began to return fire.

We could see the flashes from the automatic weapons of the defenders and Fin began to fire covering shots towards the house which was closer than I imagined it would be. I heard a groan from a guard as bullets impacted him. Another guard turned a corner firing towards me and I instinctively fired back, the impact took him off his feet and onto the floor, still and lifeless. My body was filled with adrenalin.

On the other side of the compound, two were using fire and manoeuvre to cross the largely open space from the wall to the house, one laying down fire whilst the other moved forward and the third selectively picking off the flashes bursting from the windows. Moving forward as one of the security team stepped out, gun blazing in the direction of the advancing figures, Fin thrust his MP5K out in front of him and fired a short burst that obliterated the man's face and life. Then the silence hit us. I followed Fin from room to room, the others joining us as we cleared the building, finding another 3 bodies. All we had to worry about now was finding Hans

Schröder and getting the hell out of there before the reinforcements gathered their wits and turned up.

We were moving quickly but weren't one hundred per cent sure we'd taken everyone out, so we were still guarded.

I felt the thud in my shoulder like someone had just given me a strong punch. I realised I was hit and without wanting to, down I went.

"Gene. don't move!" Fin screamed before firing back down the corridor whilst Sean O'Mulligan ran to me, firing as he did. I felt him grabbing hold of me and was dragged through the nearest open doorway. He stuffed a military field dressing, from his pocket, inside my shirt and wrapped another around my shoulder to keep it in place. He said I was fine and strangely I didn't feel too bad so I told him I could go on. Whoever had shot me had fired and retreated across a small quadrangle, the rest of the team in cautious pursuit.

It was Emilio Carballar who kicked the door into the room that lay on the opposite side but it was Gennaro Pirlo that fired the first shot, the one that struck Otto Weiss right in the center of his forehead and which dropped him like a big sack of elephant shit. In a chair behind him, sat Hans Schröder quietly waiting, seemingly unfazed by the mayhem going on all around him. At first, he addressed Fin in German, then waving a hand in dismissal he spoke in English, "I forget you Americans are ignorant of languages. So, you think you've won and that I will give you all that you require," he said, smiling in a manner clearly meant to antagonise us. Fin slapped him round the head and yanked him up from his seat with a, "I don't give a rat's ass," then dragged him towards the door.

Tape over his mouth and a hood over his head, he was restrained with zip ties and we set off back towards the gatehouse. Outside the neighbourhood was awake and trying to formulate a response. Uniformed guards, armed with clubs, milled cautiously around 50 yards away as we exited. The two 4 x 4s were positioned ready to go and as we filled them several suits arrived, weapons drawn. The uniformed security saw the way this was going to unfold and rapidly disappeared back up the street as the firing began. Two cars slid to a halt and as armed men began to get out four MP5s blazed away on fully automatic, shattering windows, pock marking bodywork and felling all before them.

"Get in the fucking vehicles!" Fin screamed as he threw the empty weapon around his back and drew his sidearm, picking off anyone still on their feet, then he was in and we screeched away, no one left in a mood to pursue us.

It seemed a long return to the chopper, made difficult for me because of the wound I'd taken and the fact that the adrenalin was fast dissipating. It was taking my breath away, exhaustion seemed to be making my legs heavy and I couldn't get anywhere near comfortable in the back. Nausea was starting to visit me and I concentrated hard to avoid spewing all over my colleagues.

At the clearing in the forest, Fin and the guys quickly swept the area to make sure it was safe and called in the Huey.

I don't remember getting into it, I must have passed out at that point but when I regained consciousness I saw Fin and Sean discussing something with repeated looks over at me. I had an awful feeling coming right across my body, an emptiness that scared me. I felt as if death was reaching a hand towards me and I thought nobody else could see.

"No," I cried out, and Emil grabbed my hand.

"You'll be fine, Eugene, we'll get you some attention as quickly as possible," he'd said but everything seemed to be like a psychedelic dream, things were moving fast around me, people also. I looked over towards Lars who's eyes were firmly set on Hans Schröder, staring directly at him with a hatred I'd not witnessed before. I felt I could see things the others couldn't. Then I must have passed out. I began dreaming, at least I thought I was, so confusing the situation around me I wasn't quite sure what was real and what wasn't.

I lay flat on straw-covered boards surrounded by others, I sensed their presence but couldn't see them, one man stood close, somehow I knew his name, Ezra Farber, he stood over me and touched my head, stroking it to calm my anxiety, my breathing seemed to ease a little and I could physically feel my heartbeat slowing down. The madness we'd been involved in seemed long ago now like time had changed somehow. I turned sideways looking for the others, they lay alongside in the grips of death, I was within a camp but felt sure it was

Auschwitz, which was strange. Ezra comforted me whilst holding the hand of a little girl with long curly blonde hair who stood next to him. "Look after him, he's my brother, we all miss him, will you tell him when you see him next," she asked and I knew exactly what she meant, it was little Anna, asking after her brother Emil. She left as soon as she'd said what she needed to and Ezra stood over my side, caring for me, making sure I didn't give into death's lure.

"You're a good man, Eugene," he said and I thought I recognised his voice but the nausea was overwhelming me once again. The next thing I knew I woke to see Emil's smiling face, "You're a good man Eugene, you can make it through," he said.

I blurted out, "Anna said they all miss you and that I'm to look after you."

Emil leant down towards me, "I knew you were a good boy Eugene, I knew you had Filip's spirit within you."

Time seemed to go missing for the next few hours as I passed in and out of consciousness, I recall Fin giving me water from a billy can and Sean injecting me with something, but I felt no pain nor emotion, it was as if it had been sucked out of me by the bullet. I had the feeling of illumination like an angel had spread its wings over me and they glowed with sunshine which warmed every part of my body.

"Hold my hand," a voice said. I put my hand out and felt a small child's hand.

"It will all be fine," Anna said and we walked down a long corridor of light, faces visible to me, they shimmered in blue, all smiling at me like they knew and had missed me, welcoming me back to their friendship after the many years we'd been parted. I knew all of them, they were my family. My father held onto me tightly and my mother wept whilst smiling, I could feel the love from each one of them, "You helped us face death, you took away the pain and fear, you gave us great comfort when we needed it the most, you're a good boy Ezra and like a bolt of lightning, I realised the man who'd so recently been my guardian was no longer *with* me, his touch of hand had passed *into* me and we became one, I was Ezra Farber and it all made sense to me. The light was intense and I became dizzy with the power of it. I wanted to stay with my family, the love was so strong.

I sat upright in a bed I was unfamiliar with. An old man with a stethoscope around his neck smiled at me and said, "Ah, welcome back. I've just given you an injection that is going to make you feel better." He packed some things into a quintessential doctor's bag. For a moment, I thought I was still dreaming. He turned to Emil and Fin. "The wound to the upper part of the right chest has torn his trapezius and subclavius muscles and also broken his collar bone. It will hurt like hell, no doubt. I've never seen someone go into shock so bad like that before but he'll be alright now."

After he'd left, Fin came back into the room. I asked him where we were. "Brick Dempsey's place. We're in Paraguay now. He owns as far as the eye can see, well, as far as you'll see when you feel well enough to get up."

He told me they had Schröder in isolation, no one had spoken to him about anything of consequence but he thought he was still in Brazil and seemed confident he'd be rescued soon and we'd all die. They were leaving him to stew a while longer.

I had a little time to contemplate my dreams, seeing the little girl Anna had been surreal, how did I recognise her and who was my guardian, Ezra Farber, and why had he passed into me. I remembered that with curiosity, some internal instinct told me he was somebody I'd known from a previous life, something I'd not contemplated before, but that's how I felt about it, maybe the trauma of the previous night had been too much for me.

The following morning, I felt much better. I was sore as hell but I was keen to re-join my colleagues and finish what we'd started. I asked Emil if I could sit in on the interview with Schröder, he said he was fine with it. But there was something else. I'd decided I had to tell him. "Emil I have something I need to tell you, it involves Lars."

"What can you possibly tell me about my friend I don't already know," he said. "It can wait, Eugene, Fin is interviewing Schröder soon."

"No, Emil, it really can't wait. Where is Lars by the way?" I asked. "He's accompanying Fin to the interview, he's one of us now, Eugene, one of the team," he said with innocence. I looked at my friend knowing what I was about to tell him would probably break his heart, but I knew I had no choice.

"Emil, Lars hasn't been honest with us," I started off.

"What do you mean?" he replied.

"You recall I went to see Stahnke before he died? I took with me some photographs I'd had taken without your knowledge. I asked Stahnke why he thought Silverman was 'The Architect' he'd spoken of. He told me it was because he'd met him in person. They'd corresponded on one of the neo-Nazi sites and Stahnke had said he really wished he could have met the man who designed the chambers and crematoria. That's how it came about. They'd had a meeting, the man he met said his name was Jonah Silverman. I showed him the photo of Silverman. I didn't tell him who it was. I just said I had two pictures of who I thought might be him. He didn't recognise it but he did recognise the other picture I had. It was Lars. When they spoke in person, Lars told him he'd designed the killing houses. He'd said he'd met Albert Speer at Auschwitz, that Speer took a shine to him when he'd told him he'd been a trainee architect before the war, before they'd rounded them all up from his home town. Speer sent him to Bełżec to assist the people there in the construction."

Emil tried to interrupt but I stopped him and went on, I had to get this terrible secret I'd kept out of me.

"The blood samples the CSI found when Max was shot, well, one of them she thought she'd messed up because there were two different DNAs in it. But she hadn't messed up. This can happen if someone has had a bone marrow transplant. At your house one day, I actually bumped into Lars in the hall, it made him drop something, a small tablet bottle and I picked it up for him but noticed as I did so the name of the medication. It was 'Prednisone', I looked it up. It's used as an immunosuppressant; people who have had a bone marrow transplant use it. When Lars flew in to meet you at the airport, something was bugging me but I brushed it aside until recently. He didn't fly in from abroad, he flew internal from Chicago. He's been in a hospital there for months, it's the best place for treating his type of cancer."

I took a breath. "Silverman was what he said he was, the accountant on the project at Bełżec and Auschwitz, it was Lars Kowalski who was 'The Architect'. I'm sorry, Emil, but it's true.

"Rubbish, Eugene, Silverman is 'The Architect' despite what he was telling us, the drugs you're on are playing games with your mind," he said to me.

"This is the hardest thing I've had to do, Emil. Lars told you lies all those years back, he was released from Auschwitz on the say-so of Albert Speer. Your paths never crossed because Lars was never in Birkenau. He designed the facilities but his superior Walter Dejaco supervised the construction and took the accolades from the SS. Lars was warned by Speer what was to come, the retribution that would be handed out. Yes, he was at Bełżec but only for the design and construction phase. Check his tattoo, Emil! They didn't tattoo people at Bełżec! They weren't there long enough. Those that were temporarily used as camp labour had their registration numbers sewn to their jackets. Lars has a tattoo, I've seen it, you must have seen it. It was only in Auschwitz they gave those tattoos."

Emil stared at me in disbelief. "All these years, I've wondered about my friend, how he survived after the war… and he lied to me."

"Do you think he could have told you the truth?"

"Is he even Lars Kowalski?" he asked, shock etched all over his face.

That I couldn't answer. "I don't know, Emil. *You* must ask him that."

He dismissed me from the room, and, somewhat strangely as it was my place of recovery, I left. He wanted to have a little time to himself. I understood the chaos going on inside his head that I was the cause of and, as I walked slowly away, I told him, "If there was a way of making this different, I would."

He replied, "I know. Please, Eugene, don't' discuss this with anyone else. I want to speak to Lars first before the others find out."

Chapter 13

The Solution

When I closed the door behind me, I saw Fin at the top of some stairs that led down to a basement. "Geno, glad you're up. C'mon, we're just about to interview Schröder. Lars has just gone down with the keys."

We'd been at it for half an hour and Schröder wasn't even admitting that's who he was. He stuck with the Wolff story, denied any connection to Forge Ore, claimed he'd been a business consultant for many firms but had been retired for years, had never been in the SS, just an ordinary soldier and he'd never been to the camps.

Fin conducted the proceedings and I could see his frustration knowing that on another day he would have wanted to shortcut everything by slapping the truth out of the tired but not yet defeated man who sat opposite him. But Fin knew it was not what we'd agreed on. We wanted full admissions, on video, something to show the world.

It was only when he produced the pictures and copies of documents from the folder beside him that I noticed a change in Hans Schröder, he sort of sagged slightly but remained defiant.

Fin: "Who did you know in the SS, Hans?"

Schröder: "I didn't know anyone in the SS. I didn't move in those circles. Of course, I saw SS men, we all did at some time or other but I didn't know any of them. And my name is Dietmar Wolff, I was in the signals and I only served in France and the Netherlands. How many times do I have to tell you?"

Fin: "Do you have cousins?"

Schröder look puzzled: "Everyone has cousins."

Fin: "Look at this, Hans." Fin slid a photograph from its cover. "This is your cousin. You remember Cousin Kurt, don't you? He tapped it with his finger. "That's your Cousin Kurt in his SS uniform." Fin leaned forward, turning the image a little and squinted at it. "In his SS Brigadeführer uniform, if I'm not mistaken."

Schröder just stared at him.

Fin: "Yeah, you remember good old cousin Kurt but he wasn't a *proper* SS man, was he? It was just an honorary title because he was worth more to your Nazi pals as a banker. In fact, he was on the board of the Bank for International Settlements." He shot me a glance acknowledging my finding that information amongst the treasures we'd downloaded from Kaspar Stahnke's computer files, before we handed them to the FBI.

Fin: "Good old cousin Kurt, he was the one who ensured you'd get all the money you needed to avoid capture and carry on the 'good' fight." He paused. "There are more, Hans. Take a look at these. They were taken at the Solahütte, the SS resort near Porabka, not too far from Auschwitz. You remember it, you spent a lovely week down there by the look of it. Look! Here's one of you with some nice female SS auxiliaries, and here's another of you with some pals. Who's are they? Don't think too hard, I'll remind you." His finger ran along the line of people. Richard Baer, Josef Mengele, Josef Kramer, Rudolf Höss *and* you. You probably don't remember it being taken but Karl Höcker, Baer's adjutant, took it. You recall Karl? You should do, because here's you and him having a few beers together. Looks like it was fun." He produced another. "Oh! Surely you'll remember this one though. It was taken from your house, one of my guys spotted it in your study when we were clearing the building. It's you. In SS uniform! How did that happen? Same face, both photos, but in the first one you'd been promoted. What have you got to say? Why did you fake the 'Final Order'?" He slammed his hand down on the table bringing Schröder back, with a jump, from wherever he was in his head.

Schröder snarled back at him, "You want to know why I did it!

I did it because I could see what was coming! I could see what the Führer could not, would not see. The war was lost. It would need a miracle and they were in very short supply. They waited for a miracle at Stalingrad and it never came. We were running out of time to rid Europe of the damned Jews. The Generals had distracted the man. I knew he would have written it sometime but I couldn't wait. We couldn't afford to wait."

Fin: "So you thought you'd help things along and speed everything up?"

Schröder smirked. "You should look at it as an act of mercy."

I could see Fin was about to lose his self-control but the moment was broken by Emil entering the room.

He just stood there, staring at Lars who was leaning against the wall in the corner, out of Schröder's line of view. I saw the look on each face and I knew the invisible information that travelled across the space between them.

I hadn't expected what happened next, I sat frozen on my chair. Lars reached behind him and pulled a gun, he must have taken it from the weapons stash and hidden it in the back of his pants. "Everyone stay just where you are, I *will* use this." He waved the weapon around then looked back at the doorway. "Emil, I'm sorry, I truly am, I know what I did and I carry my shame every day, I don't want to hurt any one of you, this is the man I've come to see." He pointed the pistol at the back of Schröder's head. "Eugene, I mean you no harm or you Fin and certainly not my friend who I owe so much to." He shrugged his shoulders. "Back away, Fin, to the door.

"Let me tell you a little story, it involves this piece of shit in front of me, you see my family were kept as hostages whilst the SS used me, Although Speer personally liked me and promised to look after my family, he trusted this man with the job. All of my family were kept separate from the other camp inmates. That promise from them secured my services. I knew exactly what I was doing and knew the consequences of my actions, I helped the Nazi's to exterminate thousands and thousands of innocents and I'm sure that God will punish me for my actions much more than I have myself." He turned Schröder's head to face him."You should have kept them safe, but you didn't. They were put on the list for the chambers in the last of the killings and when someone brought it to your attention you said, 'What does it matter, they are just Jews, leave them on the list'. How do I know this? I found the person who showed you the list, quite by accident. He told me your words and said when he tried to remind you of what *you* had promised Speer you simply said, 'Fuck Speer' and left. Your only thought at the end was for yourself. I've waited for this moment all of my life, you've had a good life, a life you are not worthy of, one which has given you riches you stole from the dead and dying. With a click of your fingers, you controlled our lives, to live or die was the power you had over people." He pushed the gun into Schröder's cheek.

"Are you afraid?" he asked.

"Of you and your kind? " Schröder spat out. "You're no better than rats, you deserved it. And you? You knew what you were doing, you snivelling swine. I was there when you begged Speer on your knees to save your pathetic family. They had some value for a time but when you'd finished, especially with those final exquisite touches, there was only going to be one result. You people were so gullible."

We watched Lars, transfixed. He was trembling, tears streaming down his cheeks. Suddenly, he smashed the pistol into Schröder's face tearing a gash that bled freely and dragged him from the chair to the floor, Schröder raising his bound hands trying to protect himself. Fin stepped forward, an unlikely protector, but we wanted this Nazi alive. Lars stabbed the gun at him. "Get back, Fin. I *will* kill you if I have to."

No matter what I thought of Schröder, it still wasn't a pleasant sight, seeing an old man treated in such a way. I thought we were better than that, but then my family hadn't been murdered in the Holocaust.

Lars told him to get to his knees. In a strangely calm manner, he told him quietly, "I'm not like you, none of us were. If you beg me for mercy, I will give it to you. That is the difference between us. Beg for my mercy and live or die now."

I'm not sure why, maybe because of his arrogance and defiance, I expected Schröder to refuse and goad Lars to the end but he didn't. He began to sob, fighting for breath between each one, and I found myself, momentarily, feeling sorry for him.

Tears cascaded down his face, he held his bound hands in front of him as if in prayer. We did nothing, frozen by the moment.

"No, please. It was the war. I was only following Speer's orders." He sucked in more air, the words coming faster now. "He wasn't the man you thought he was. He told me, privately, that when I had finished with your talents it would be fitting to burn you and your family in crematoria you designed, Please, have mercy on me, I did my best but I had to follow orders. Please, don't kill me." More deep sobbing, mucus dripped from his nose and more tears, so many that he couldn't see Lars was no longer in front of him. "Please! I beg for your mercy."

"Who's gullible now," Lars whispered in his ear, from behind then shot him through the back of the head, blood spraying out from his face over the floor and table. Schröder flopped to one side and was still.

Lars looked up at us. "I'm sorry, Emil. I love you like a brother but I helped to kill so many people," he said and placed the gun in his mouth. "Oh, Jesus!" Emil screamed as the shot rang out. "No!!"

The Architect was dead.

Epilogue

Lars Kowalski was laid to rest in the Long Island crematorium.

Some men are born evil, some are made to be. Lars Kowalski had been the best friend Emil ever had and endured what he had himself, passing judgement on him was the easy option, but who was I to do that. It's hard to judge a man's actions after fifty years of torment. His wife, Panni, had died some years ago from tuberculosis, most likely brought about from the death camp. He'd struggled and battled through leukemia, it seemed with one aim in mind. Hundreds of people died of disease in the camps, some carried their illnesses through the remainder of their lives, as I assumed Panni had.

He had reason to hate the Nazis but I just couldn't believe his role in the camps. I tried to even the crimes up, blaming the way Hans Schröder had killed his family after using him for the Nazi's benefit but it was hard. Emil's family were murdered by them and probably every night's sleep he'd had in the last fifty years was filled with images of Auschwitz and the gas chambers we now knew his friend Lars had helped to design and build.

Although the evidence I'd gathered told me something was seriously wrong, I didn't really want to come to the obvious conclusion. I'd been in denial, even up to the moment he said those words himself, "I'm sorry."

I held out a hope I'd somehow got it wrong, but I hadn't.

On closer inspection of the Sikora files, it turned out Aleksy Markowski had interviewed Lars many years ago, suspecting him to be The Architect but he just couldn't make the case so he left the Albert Speer book with the initials inscribed within the folders as a reminder of a lost cause, or perhaps a future clue.

I remembered the words Emil had told me, the ones Alexsy had told him, "Don't go chasing lost causes, you'll waste too much time going round in circles." I said it out loud and Emil added through a sad smile, "This time my old friend was wrong. It's the continuous solution."

We'd buried Schröder in the forest, bodybagged Lars and took a long ride back in a DC-4 courtesy of Brick Demspey and, I suspected, his CIA pals who had a whole 'thing' going on in Paraguay and were 'heading that way anyway'.

Lars left a note explaining everything and Emil kept hold of it, following his wishes, still remembering him as the young man who'd been through as much hell as he had himself. It could quite easily have been Emil, but he'd not surrendered his spirit; he'd met Luiza and attempted to put that life away in a box.

We all stood outside the crematorium waiting for the ceremony to begin. Emil nudged me and subtly pointed to a nearby fence. There it was, a small colourful bird, a 'Sikora', preening its feathers then watching us.

Emil said, quietly. "I was expecting you to be here. Yes, my time will come and you'll be there waiting for me, helping me to the next life. But, you know I still have important work to do, so, tell me, are you going to give me the time, old friend?"

The 'Sikora' tilted its head from side to side as if considering the matter, broke into song and flew off.

Emil caught my eye and said with a little smile, "I think we're good for a while yet, Eugene."

The Sweet Water Tales

The Blink of an Eye

Into the Blue

Operation Homecoming

The Sikora Files

The Auschwitz Protocol

The Architect

Printed in Great Britain
by Amazon